SEX DEATH ROCK N ROLL 2
The Russell Aquarius Edition

Short stories based on the feature film
"The Second Age of Aquarius"

by

BROOKE LEWIS BELLAS
NANCY LONG
MARTIN OLSON
DARREN GORDON SMITH
STACI LAYNE WILSON

praise for
SEX DEATH ROCK N ROLL
PART ONE

"Anyone can write about rock n roll, but when you get heavy-hitters like Staci Layne Wilson and Darren Gordon Smith applying their combined knowledge of the genre for our entertainment, you know you're in for a rare treat. And what a treat it is. Electrifying, terrifying, and unique. I loved every minute I spent in these dark, deranged worlds. Bring on the sequel!" – Kealan Patrick Burke, Bram Stoker Award-winning Author 'Kin' and 'The Turtle Boy'

"Uniquely nightmarish. There's a touch of Bret Easton Ellis in the stories' surreal mix of anxiety, satire, and obsessive pop music analysis and inventory." – Don Mancini, Saturn-award winning Writer 'Child's Play' films and 'Hannibal' TV series

"Tales of the fantastic blended with the razor kiss of rock n roll." – Tristan Risk, Burlesque Icon 'Little Miss Risk'

"Like a great rock song, this book stays in your head long after you finish it. Funny, macabre and fascinating!" – Jace Anderson, Co-Writer 'Mother of Tears' and 'Fractured' films

"With backstories like these – Wilson's dad is a rockstar (The Ventures), Smith is a musician (*Repo! The Genetic Opera*) – their stories have to be great. And they are!" Bobby Smithe, Author 'Bowie Bible'

"Fiery and fevered scribes Staci Layne Wilson and Darren Smith have delivered an anthology book devoted to rock n roll fuelled short stories which read as lyrical as the songs and music they pay tribute to. With an authentic and un-compromising dedication to musicians from decades past, Wilson and Smith deliver a highly energetic and equally nuanced set of stylish tales of obsession, cynicism, neurosis and rage – all driven by a street sensibility and catapulting from the varied voices of the angry outsider. Not to be missed!" – Lee Gambin, Author 'We Can Be Who We Are: Movie Musicals From the 70s'

contents
SEX DEATH ROCK N ROLL 2
The Russell Aquarius Edition

- - - - - - - - - - - - - -

About the Authors
About the Film

ROCK PAPER SCISSORS

By Brooke Lewis Bellas & Staci Layne Wilson

You may remember Tawny Stevens. She was a video vixen for a hot minute in 1991. No, she's not the redheaded babe who rolled around provocatively on the hood of a sports car—that was the '80s. Our Tawny is a brunet, and she isn't notorious like the other one, either; she is a low-profile entrepreneur and even has her own small but well-regarded line of hair spray and mousse. It's called S.W.A.K. (sealed with a kiss).

I met her on assignment for *Rolling Stone*. I guess that's what you'd call a full-circle moment, considering that one of my first freelance jobs was to follow Russell Aquarius on his tour of famous U.S. battlefields in 1970. Yes, I've been at this for quite a while.

When I was sent to Asbury Park, New Jersey, I was less-than-impressed. My assignments these days—as a so-called elder statesman—usually involve jet-setting with Sting on his private plane as we fly over the Bahamas or maybe even playing video games with Lana Del Rey in the Hollywood Hills. But not this time. They sent me out to interview a has-been who never really was. I mean, does appearing in a barely-released Bon Jovi video even qualify one for a spread in the world's foremost music magazine? Probably not. But hey—I'm a correspondent, and I report on whatever the readers (and my editor) dictate.

The real reason my editor wanted me to talk to her is because she's the mother of Alberta Stevens, the innovative computer-programmer who stunned the world by bringing back the "Furry Freak" himself, Russell Aquarius, from the Great Beyond.

For you in the back: Aquarius was poised for major stardom in 1970, but his life was short-circuited by a faulty microphone and an ill-timed rainstorm during his mini-tour of famous American battlefields. And this was *after* a crazed groupie tried to blind the acid-rocker with, ironically, battery acid.

Aquarius is a survivor, though—fifty-odd years after joining the so-called "27 Club" (famous folks to die at that exact age are oddly in abundance in the music world), he was jolted back to life by Tawny's daughter through an avatar she created. Now Aquarius is more famous than he ever would have been had he lived a natural life cycle. Like good old Neil sang, "It's better to burn out than fade away." Little did anyone know, it is possible to burn out, fade away, then come back and blaze brightly for all eternity.

While Aquarius enjoys fame on his "Never-ending Cosmic Tour" (catch it on RussellAquarius.com for a hefty fee), his *alleged* creator, Alberta Stevens, hedges on whether or not she actually made that avatar (for the record, I think she did—and clearly, so does my editor or I wouldn't be writing an article about her mom… the younger Ms. Stevens has refused any and all interviews).

I must admit to a personal bias here. I was actually there on the scene when Russell was electrocuted. I'd been following him on that tour while on assignment, and though it was my job to report on everything, I did not admit then how much it shook me. I was younger than Russell, and thought I was invincible—until I saw that. It actually wasn't the first death I'd witnessed… those were some pretty wild times… but it hit me hard. My drinking and drugging (hey, it was the '70s) went on for a while after that, but with a lot less gusto and bravado. I'd glimpsed my own mortality through the demise of someone I liked and genuinely admired. I cleaned up my act, and I changed almost everything about myself, including how I wrote and what I wrote about. But rock 'n roll is in my soul, and I never forgot my roots.

But I digress. This assignment became more intriguing to me after I suggested to my editor that I interview not only Alberta's mom, but those who know her best. So far, I've only got a landlady, an ex-boyfriend, and her former boss at Muzi-Tech, but it's a start.

I landed in Newark, which is the nearest airport at a mind-numbing fifty-six miles from Asbury Park. Tawny insisted on picking me up at the airport herself. I refused at first, but the woman's hospitality would not be derailed. Part of my reluctance had to do with professionalism—how could I be an objective journalist if she picked me up and made me feel indebted to her? I drew the line at her offer to sleep in her spare bedroom, though.

The first thing that struck me, as she helped me stuff my overnight bag into the nearly nonexistent trunk of her bright red Corvette, was how tiny she is. At five-foot nothing, I think most of her height is made up of high heels and teased hair. She hugged me in welcome and gave me the biggest smile I'd seen in months. (I live in Manhattan, and as you may know, New Yorkers are not known for their grins and giggles.)

I later learned she was only seventeen—and unwed—when she became a mom, but still she looked like she could be Alberta's slightly elder sister. Gotta love good genes. And jeans. Tawny's Z Cavaricci acid wash tapered trousers fit her like a glove, and she wore an extra-small original Def Leppard tour tee that just barely covered her extra-large boobs. Her perfume was Poison by Dior, I believe—but I couldn't be sure, as I hadn't caught a whiff of that stuff in the past thirty years.

"Hi, doll! How was your flight? Was it First Class? Did they give you champagne?" Her questions were more rapid-fire than an Yngwie Malmsteen guitar solo.

They didn't stop, even as we settled into the tiny cockpit of her car. "Can I get you anything? You've gotta be starvin! Jeet?" My brain strained as it worked to decipher her Jersey accent. She repeated: "Didja eat? There's a sub in the glovebox,"—I'm not kidding: a footlong Blimpie was wedged inside—"or we can stop at Dunkin Donuts for a coffee!" Or as she said it, *Cawfee.*

"No, no, I'm good, thanks."

I wanted to get right down to business and start recording, but she laughed me off.

"Oh, my gawd, you reporters! Always on the job. Take a load off. We got all the time in the world for that. And don't forget, I'm takin you back to the airport. I will *not* take no for an answer."

On the drive, we listened to a mix of '80s rock, and she reminisced about all the bands she got to see live back in the day ("Thanks to my fake I.D.!") and through the early '90s ("Even after Alberta came along. She was my little wingman!").

We made it to Tawny's hometown in a little over an hour. Asbury Park is a "charming" mix of shopping centers, amusement parks, Italian delis, ageing Mustang GTs, and residents walking around in velour jogging suits and sneakers.

Her home was cozy and smelled of baked goods… mixed with hair products and perfume. "Is this where Alberta was raised?" I asked, looking around at the cluttered décor. In its own way, it looked like a mom's house should (even though Tawny was a knockout, she had a definite maternal air about her).

"Oh, no, hon. For the first few years of her life, we lived with my mother. In fact, it was Ma who made Alberta the Russell Aquarius fan she is to this day." Tawny chuckled at the memory. "I gotta say… I still don't know why she freakin loves that hippie music so much. When I was younger, I listened to the hottest bands—Poison, Skid Row, Great White. Even Stryper! I loved Kiss, that's really what S.W.A.K. stands for, and of course, our local boys, Bon Jovi. Oh! Have I got a Bon Jovi story for *you*!" She stopped suddenly, seeming to think better of what she was about to say.

"Go on," I coaxed. I knew she was in one of their videos, of course. But a "story" could be good.

No luck. "Oh! I better shut my big mouth," she said, putting her leopard-print purse down on the red leather sofa. "I promised Alberta I'd behave myself for this interview."

"May I ask why *she* won't give any interviews?"

"You wanna drink?" Tawny asked brightly, her hazel eyes twinkling.

I looked at the time on my phone. "Well, it must be five o'clock somewhere!" I shrugged. Drinking on the job already. My younger self would be shaking his head at this fussy fogey—my first assignment, on the band The Near-Death Experience, involved an actual death. And drinks. And drugs. But that's another story. I'm saving it for my memoir.

Now I was intrigued, and I was silently determined to get that secret story out of Tawny before the evening ended.

She took my overnight bag to the spare room and called out, "Make yourself at home, get comfy. I'll grab the JD."

Spare room? *Hm. I guess I'm staying here, after all. And JD as in Jack Daniels?* "Um," I protested, "Do you have anything more… daytime friendly?"

She crossed through the living room into the kitchen. "How about a Zima?"

Zima? Did they still make that stuff? I decided I'd better stick to wine, if she had any. Still politely joining in, but not getting schnockered. It's all about balance; that's my motto. "I'd love a white wine, if you have any."

Tawny didn't reply, but I heard glass bottles clanging together as she presumably rummaged for the lighter stuff.

Her home was colorful and bold. There were crimson color pops everywhere and leopard-pattern was clearly a favorite—borderline bordello, by way of a mom's sensibilities. There were several framed family photos crowded together on a narrow console table—her daughter's senior class picture was blown up and took center stage.

I knew, from the scant details publicly available, that Tawny had put herself through beauty school while raising Alberta. And now she owned a small chain of salons called Rock, Paper, Scissors. The logo featured a classic '80s flying-v electric guitar and a stylized sketch of Tawny gesturing with hand-horns. Then there was the hair spray and mousse line, so she'd made something of herself.

Tawny returned with a serving tray balancing a bottle of Jack Daniels No. 7, two shot glasses—"Just in case you change your mind, doll"—and a stemless glass filled with ice and white wine. I took my drink with thanks as she set the tray down on the coffee table.

I gestured to a framed portrait of a chic and stylish older woman. "Is that your mother?"

Tawny went to the photo and picked it up, gazing at the image for a moment before putting it back down. She nodded. "That's Ma. Or Nana, as Alberta called her." She sat down beside me on the sofa, then took a shot, leaving a neon pink lipstick print on the rim. "Thank gawd for her. I woulda just *died* without her! She raised Alberta too, you know."

"I didn't know," I replied. I got out my phone. "Mind if we start now?" She gave the nod, and I swiped to the recording app. "Please, go on."

"Well, this whole Russell Aquarius business started with Ma. While I was puttin myself through beauty school and workin two parttime jobs, Alberta spent a ton of time with her Nana. We all lived together in a two-bedroom walkup, and there wasn't even a view!" She sighed. Oh, the indignity. "Daddy had passed the year before." She crossed herself. "I'm tellin you, that's why I acted out at such a young age. I'd just turned seventeen when I was in that Bon Jovi video, but I had a fake I.D. I got it down in Philly on South Street."

"Were you in high school at the time?"

She nodded. "But I was ditchin, at least twice a week, to hit the Jersey Shore. Gawd, how we loved the boardwalk, the beach, the rides, and those games where you could win a big stuffed bear or a plastic ring. At night, my girlfriends and I would hitch a ride with guys in bands, to watch them play. We freakin loved The Stone Pony. And I still go to The Wonder Bar here in town, for yappy hour." Her eyes brightened. "We should go there later!" I nodded. Maybe. If I got my story. "I do like a good party, and I started young," she said.

"You don't say!" I laughed. "Same here," I told her, in hopes of forging common ground and gaining her trust.

"I know! You were a kid when you started writin for *Rolling Stone?*"

I nodded but didn't elaborate. I was little surprised that she knew my history, but I wanted Tawny to stick to telling *her* story. "The video. Is that when you met Alberta's dad?"

She gave a smirky grin, and shook her head. "Oh, no, Mr. Lightfoot, I promised Alberta I'd behave. I ain't spillin *any* family secrets."

"I get it," I said agreeably. "And please—call me Gabe."

"Gabe." She took a small sip of her drink, then curled her legs beneath her, getting comfortable. "I always dreamed of bein a video vixen," she sighed. She said the words with the same reverence other people might say *doctor* or *lawyer*. "Ever since MTV started. I was only six or seven then, but oh, how I would dance and rock out to all the videos! Remember when videos actually told freakin stories? Like Cyndi Lauper's *Girls Just Wanna Have Fun*, or Madonna's *Papa Don't Preach*." Her eyes flicked downward. "Well, that one hit a little close to home." Then she gave a wistful smile. "No regrets, though. And Daddy had passed by the time... well, you know. Even though Alberta wasn't planned, havin her was one of my best decisions ever. In a way, she was the daughter my mom never had. Alberta loved Russell's music, she was a straight-A student, and she never, ever *tawked* back. They spent hours together listenin to music, talkin, and bakin biscotti."

"No!" I interjected. "You're making that last one up."

"I ain't!" Tawny protested, laughing. "We're *very* Italian. Anyway, Alberta was always very smart. When she was ten, all she wanted for her birthday was a Treo."

I cocked my head. "A trio? Of what?"

"That's what *I* said! But no, it was a smartphone. It did almost everythin they do now. Totally cuttin-edge. Of course, it was an expensive gift for a little girl. But she wasn't your typical kid."

"Let's back up a little bit. How did the audition for Bon Jovi come about? What was it like to shoot that video?"

"Well, as I told you, I loved music videos. *Loved!* They were *everything* to me. I wanted to be one of the Robert Palmer *Addicted to Love* girls, or on that sailboat in Duran Duran's *Rio*! That's where I got all my beauty tips and fashion sense. I learned so much about clothes, makeup, and of course, hair." She primped her locks for emphasis, then went on. "I'd seen Bon Jovi live, like, forty-seven times. Oh, my gawd, they played at The Stone Pony all the time. I had such a crush on... um," She took another shot. "Alec!"

That one took me by surprise. Not Jon, not Ritchie. And a *bass player* at that! No one crushes on the bass player. And I couldn't help but notice the pause before she said his name. I didn't mention it, though—a long career as an interviewer has taught me that people feel compelled to fill silences. The less I say, the more they do. I thought for a moment, remembering in the course of my research that Alec never had any kids. *Or did he?* Hmmm.

Tawny took the bait but didn't swallow it. Without elaborating any further on specific band members, she said, "I got to know the road crew and their manager, and a couple of guys from their openin act at The Stone Pony, The Bingenheimers."

Oh, wow. Talk about a blast from the past. The Bingenheimers. Good lord! The band members all dressed like the famously oddball DJ from L.A., Rodney Bingenheimer—plus they had his trademark pageboy haircut with spikes at the top, and they never smiled.

Tawny went on. "It was just a lucky break that I happened to be in the club when they were filmin that video. Well, maybe not… I mean, I was there all the freakin time. I wish I could have been in the video longer. I coulda had a career. You know, like Courtney Cox in *Dancin in the Dark*. Oh, yeah—I saw Bruce live, too. Only nineteen times, though; he was too classic rock for my taste, more Ma's and Alberta's speed. I loved glitz and glam, Spandex and sparkles, leather and lace. I still do!"

I nodded; I could sure see that. "I recently revisited your video on YouTube. Terrible copy. Looked like it was ripped from an 8th generation VHS." The song was from an unpopular, pretty much forgotten B-side, so that was the only upload I could find. "I think I spotted you in the crowd, but are you in the backstage scene at all?" That was the bit where the groupies—excuse me, *video vixens*— come popping out of big cakes and giant bottles of champagne, wearing little more than red Bonnie Bell lip-gloss and Lee press-on nails.

"I was, but they freakin cut me out when they found out how old I really was," she rolled her eyes. Then she brightened. "It's all good, though. They forgot, or never noticed, that I'm *featured* in the audience, too. So, I'm still in there! Ha!"

"Clearly, the women in your family are drawn to rock music."

"Oh, yeah. Ma went to so many concerts with Daddy when they were datin. And even after they married, and you know, *did it*. They saw Russell Aquarius, of course, and The Doors, Iron Butterfly, The Strawberry Alarm Clock. You name it! I still have some of her records here. That's how she kept Alberta entertained whenever I had to work overtime—Alberta loved to watch those LPs spin around and around. She was seven when she took apart Ma's record player and put it back together again. She's the smartest person I know. She was always wantin to know what made things tick."

"I guess that's what makes her such an incredible programmer." I took a small sip of my drink, pacing myself. "Not that I know much about computers. But her Russell Aquarius avatar is light years ahead of the technology we have today. She should be proud. Why do you think she doesn't want to talk about it?"

Tawny's eyes glinted and she gave me some classic mom-style side-eye. She was onto me. "Who said she created that avatar? I mean, I saw some stories on the news, but I ain't sayin a word. Anyway, she's always been a shy girl. She doesn't like the spotlight. Crazy, huh? Maybe that's my fault. I threw her right into the action as a kid. I'd take her with me to beauty school sometimes, and instead of usin that Farrah Fawcett lookin head we all had, the students would practice on Alberta! She never seemed to mind much, even when my friend Marilyn—she works with me now, by the way—dyed her hair purple. Don't worry: it was a temporary Manic Panic rinse, and totally safe. But still, Alberta didn't want to go outside for a week! Maybe that's what led to…"

"To what?"

"Oh, never mind. Anyway, she liked to stay in her room and do her computer stuff. She never did sneak out of the house like I did. Sometimes… oh, this is *bad*, but it was sooo fun… I'd tell Ma I was spendin the weekend with one of my friends, and my friend would tell her parents the same thing, that she was at mine. But instead, we'd sneak over to Philly to go to The Spectrum, or to New York to CBGB. I saw so many bands! I was kind of a wild child."

"That's an excellent way to become a professional milk carton model," I quipped.

"Oh, Gabe! You are *too* funny. But you've used that one before. In the March 1992 issue of *Glam Rock*. You did an article on Faster Pussycat, and you said most of their groupies were so young and so wild, they'd probably end up as milk carton models."

I cocked a brow. *Impressive.* "So, I see you did your homework. You vetted me, did you?"

She shrugged. "No, I've been readin your stories for years. I used to collect *Rolling Stone, Creem, Hit Parader, The Village Voice*, and, well, all the rock mags and even some of the underground zines. I still have most of them crated up in the basement. I always liked how you wrote. Nicer than Lester Bangs, funnier than Dave Marsh, and more relatable than Ellen Willis."

Hm. A connoisseur of rock journalism. My preconceived notions of Tawny were being reassessed and reframed.

Tawny stood, then wobbled. She'd put away a lot of Jack Daniels for such a little lady. She steadied, then declared, pointing, "I wanna ask you somethin!"

It sounded more like an accusation than a pre-question. "Okay…" I agreed, somewhat warily.

"Well, there's this article you wrote about Lemmy Esposito. You remember?" She pronounced it *remem-bah.*

How could I forget? He was the lead singer and guitarist of The Bingenheimers, the band she mentioned mere moments ago. They opened for Bon Jovi for three months in '91, then they broke up. The world at large had forgotten the ill-fated musician by now, but he was hot stuff for a hot minute. I was one of the few to ever publish a full profile on him. That was another good reason for me to *remem-bah.* It was a cover story, in fact—which had come as a surprise to me since he was only on the precipice of stardom and not yet a *bona fide* star.

Kind of like Russell Aquarius, but a couple of decades later. Only he wasn't electrocuted by a microphone. He disappeared.

Tawny wobbled toward the kitchen. "I have that magazine in the basement. I'm gonna go get it because I wanna ask you somethin…"

I got up to follow her. There was no way I was going to allow the intoxicated woman to attempt steep, downward basement stairs in those Lucite stilts she was wearing without assistance. As it turned out, she didn't need any help.

The basement was finished, and thoughtfully organized. Several crates filled with records, CDs, rock memorabilia, and magazines were stacked to one side. Tawny made a beeline for a certain one, and after minimal rifling, she found the copy of *Glam Rock* boasting my cover story. Unlike the other issues, this one was inside a protective clear plastic envelope.

I also saw some old monitors, towers, and keyboards. Who kept old computer stuff lying around? Proud moms, that's who. I indicated the hardware. "Alberta's?"

Tawny nodded and smiled wistfully. "Hard to believe those things are worthless now. And the software. Oh, my gawd! When Alberta turned thirteen, I gave her a PowerBook somethin-or-other, loaded with all the newest programs and games. It cost me a fortune." She wiped at a tear. Then she chuckled, catching my expression. "I'm not cryin about the money, silly." She put her free hand on my elbow. "Come on, let's get back upstairs. This room makes me feel too sentimental."

That was exactly what I wanted. I could feel the faint electronic hum of the recording iPhone in my front pocket. But she'd already started up the stairs, so I followed. She was steady now, perhaps sobered by the memories in the basement.

As we settled back on her red leather couch, she started to take the magazine from its protective sleeve. But I didn't want to go off-topic. I was here to talk about Tawny, and (especially) Alberta. "Tell me why you got emotional when you saw your daughter's old computers."

Tawny stood up. "Would you wanna a wooder?"

"Huh?"

"Wooder."

"Oh! Water," I realized. "Sure."

She went into the kitchen and quickly returned with two plastic bottles of Zydrate water. *Hydrate with Zydrate*, their jingle went. I could tell Tawny was stalling, but she was not getting off the hook now. She handed me mine, then took a pull of hers. Before she could try to change the subject, I repeated my question.

"Well, Alberta was such a mature little girl. An old soul, Ma called her. She would worry about me, workin so freakin much. But thirteen is such an important birthday, and she really wanted that computer. So I took on an extra night shift, graveyard, after her bedtime, so I could buy it for her. But I knew she'd feel bad about that, so I told her she won it. I said I entered her in some contest, so that way, she could just enjoy the gift and not worry about me."

I remembered how hard my own parents had worked to support me, and how I felt like I'd let them down when I quit school to become a gypsy rock and roll writer, off touring with bands for most of the year. But like Tawny with Alberta, they supported my dream. Now *my* eyes were threatening to tear up.

Tawny caught my look, patted my knee, and then she opened the magazine to my spread on Lemmy Esposito. It was one of the most in-depth pieces I'd ever done at the time, and I even took the pictures. Not the one on the cover, though. Mick Rock took that one. The image showed him holding his one-of-a-kind transparent guitar, which was actually a fully-realized computer that he designed himself—it wrote new songs based on algorithms from how his fingers moved on the strings. The guitar, still the only one in existence, stands on display at the Rock and Roll Hall of Fame in Cleveland.

"I've read this article 214 times," Tawny said. "But one thing I've never been able to verify was what you said about his girlfriend. I didn't know he had a girlfriend," she said. "I never saw her at any of the shows."

"Not a girlfriend, exactly," I clarified.

"A hookup? Did he say that?" Tawny's face took on an inscrutable expression.

"No… more like someone he loved, but she didn't know how he felt, and he was going into rehab again, so he asked me not to publish her name."

"What was her name?"

"I shouldn't say. Besides, he disappeared ages ago. What does any of this matter anymore? He probably changed his name and became a salesman or something."

"No, he didn't," Tawny blurted.

"Oh?"

"Ummm…" She smiled deviously. "Tell me her name, and maybe I'll tell ya what *really* happened to Lemmy."

Maybe. Didn't sound like a fair deal to me, but it was ancient history anyway. "Antonia."

Tawny's eyes widened. "That's *me!*"

My jaw dropped. Of course, Tawny couldn't be her real name. Who'd name a sweet, newborn baby something so tawdry? So, it made sense: Antonia, Toni, Tawny.

"I was born Antonia Stefania Sophia Santaluciano. I changed over to Stevens when I got married—it only lasted six days, but I kept his name." She set her water aside and, as if mentioning her brief marriage set her off, she slammed two back-to-back shots of Jack Daniels.

She handed me one, but I refused it. This could be big, and I needed a clear head. What if Lemmy Esposito, the computer-guitar playing burnout, was Alberta's dad? If so, and I broke the news, I'd be getting another cover story for sure!

Then I noticed Tawny was quietly weeping. It seemed I'd turned into the Barbara Walters of rock reporters.

"I'm so happy, I'm freakin out," Tawny said. "He *did* care about me. He said he loved me, really?"

I nodded. "And you say you know what happened to him?"

Tawny sniffled loudly, then composed herself. "I only got one letter from him, after he left. It was postmarked Tibet. He ditched rehab and flew directly to the Phugtal"—she pronounced it *fuck-it-all*—Buddhist Monastery."

Holy shit! I'd actually been there once, when I was doing an undercover story in the early '70s on Ringo Starr. He'd gone there, too, for so-called enlightenment. I think all he did was shave his beard and get high on esoteric psychedelics, though. They called it "drug-induced ego dissolution." (Or D.I.E.D. for short; kind of ironic, if you ask me.)

Anyway, the monastery is tucked away in the remote Lungnak Valley in south-eastern Zanskar, in the Himalayan region of Ladakh, in Northern India, and its carved into the face of a sheer cliff. It was a bitch to get to—even now, it can only be reached on foot or by mountain donkey, and during winter, the monks' supplies have to be ferried across the frozen Zanskar River by dogs pulling a sled. Their food and drugs are packed inside insulated crates. That's how I smuggled myself in to get the exclusive on Ringo. But that's another story for the memoirs.

Tawny claimed that she didn't have the letter anymore, but she said it was definitely from Lemmy.

She recognized his handwriting, and he said he wanted to write to her before he took his Vow of Illiteracy. After that, he could only dictate to a scribe. And after his Vow of Silence kicked in, he couldn't even do that. "He said he was sorry he had to go, and…"

…And that's it.

I played a game of rock-paper-scissors with myself after I listened to the rest of what she had to say, when she asked me to keep her secrets. Rock may crush scissors, but scissors cut paper, and I'm not going to print it.

Is Lemmy Esposito Alberta's father? Or is it the man who made Tawny the short-term Mrs. Stevens? You may guess, but it might not be what you think. Did Alberta singlehandedly bring Russell Aquarius back to life? Probably. But who can say for sure? Not me.

I have come to respect Tawny, and I believe she and her family deserve their privacy. The story's still fun anyway, don't you agree? It's all about balance.

After our interview concluded, Tawny took me to yappy hour at The Wonder Bar and we danced the night away.

I even had a shot of JD.

OLD SOUL AND ASSHOLE

By Darren Gordon Smith

D. Gordon Smitty, *El Taupinata Tribune Staff Reporter*

For many of us, Monday mornings are something to dread. After two measly days of enjoying your life, the alarm goes off, and you're immediately thrown into the icy lake of the workday world and desperately swimming to a distant shore. But that shore is work, either at an office or at home, and online. Yeah, it's grim.

But that's not the way Roger Van Vliet, age 71, sees things, and he's no morning person. He may be tired but he's thankful when another Monday morning rears its ugly, misbegotten head. "Every day above ground," he tells me, "Is a bonus day."

Van Vliet, a retired history teacher in El Taupinata, California, has reason to be happy. Two years ago, he dodged a bullet.

Literally.

It happened early one cold February. It was a typical chilly morning, he recalls, when a brilliant sunrise lit up the Taupinata Valley, refracting its orange glow through the tulle fog, a time when it seems like the only people up and walking are either derelicts or annoying overachievers. Van Vliet was rolling eastbound in his pickup truck on the way to a building project he volunteered to help with. He would've preferred an extra hour or two of sleep but he knew he'd have to get to the job site before the regular mass of anti-Socialist demonstrators blocked the gates again in their misguided efforts to stop People for Places from building more affordable homes.

But first, Roger had to grab a bite to eat. And for him, that meant onion rings. Lots of them. And that meant Jack in the Box. He pulled into one he'd been going to so many times that month that Gretchen, the cheerful teen at the drive-thru pickup window, always asked him if he wanted his "usual."

That morning, he drove up to the belly of the Jack beast to place four orders of those mouth-watering golden browned rings. But as he pulled toward the pickup window, he noticed a guy in a scraped metal GTO in front of him screaming at the drive-thru cashier.

Roger rolled down his window to hear what the hubbub was about. Apparently, the guy in the beat-up muscle car was angry about the pickles in his burger. They were either too crisp, or not soggy enough; Roger doesn't remember exactly what the guy's beef was. The guy threw his burger at the girl, which stuck to the drive-up window. Roger saw Gretchen's chipper smile fade. Her face was red.

Meanwhile, a car rolled up right behind Roger's in the drive-thru line and started to honk and flash its high-beams. Roger turned around. The lady in the driver's seat was sitting patiently, seemingly lost in thought, but the guy in the death seat next to her was slapping the horn and telling everybody in front of them to hurry the fuck up.

Then Roger heard a muffled cry coming through the intercom system. That was too much for him. He got out of his truck to see if Gretchen was alright.

No sooner had he stepped out when he felt the cold steel gauge pushed right up to his lips. The size felt like a Colt .45.

"I'll shoot this geezer from mouth to ass if I don't get my food just the way I like it," Van Vliet recalls the angry pickle guy yelling to the poor girl as he cocked the gun in his face. In his long career as an educator, Roger, of course, had witnessed scores of student shootings, but this was the closest he had come to death.

Just then, from Roger's sideline view, the honking jerk from the car behind him got out and started toward the gunman, cursing and growling along the way. Roger remembers the jerk yelling to the angry pickle man, "Listen to me, little gun-fuck, I just spent two years stuck inside a phone and I'm not about to let some dickass redneck hold up my strawberry shake!"

Roger stiffens as he recounts this terrifying time. "Suddenly, I heard a BOOM BOOM BOOM…and then, just pindrop silence."

The next thing Roger saw was strawberry shake jerk and angry pickle dude both lying dead at the drive-thru in conjoining circles of blood. Roger was later told by authorities that his savior –the shake jerk, that is - had run out of his car, tripped on the curb and fell towards the gunman. Though the CCTV footage of the incident is about as blurry as free porn at a Motel 6, it shows the gunman calmly aiming and shooting the Good Samaritan jerk with the expertise of a skeet shooter.

The altercation and shooting gave Gretchen a split second to call for help. She knew that the local cops would do nothing without a hefty contribution to their "benevolence" fund, and the restaurant's failure to put up a "Blue Lives Matter" sign would antagonize them further. Instead, she made an emergency call to her childhood friend at the McDonald's next-door. Her friend (who asked not to be named) guided the franchise's armed drone that they keep on hand, to the Jack drive-thru, where it hovered for a couple seconds before shooting the madman dead.

Roger was credited for helping to save Gretchen's life. But for him, the credit belongs to the hothead in the car behind him and Gretchen's quick thinking. "But please don't call me a hero," he says with a shy smile, "I was just *really* hungry for onion rings."

2.

We're sitting at Roger's kitchen table, sipping iced coffee while he shows me a dozen dog-eared and yellowing old pics and reams of paper with his hieroglyphic–like notes. He tells me that not long after the incident, he drove back to the restaurant expressed his gratitude to Gretchen. These days, he tutors her to prepare for her SATs and has offered to pay her future college tuition.

He also planned to thank his Good Samaritan's next of kin, too - if he had any - as well as the woman who had driven him. But, besides the name provided by one of the police officers at the scene—Julio del Toro - this was all he had to go on.

That wasn't a whole lot, says Roger. "I found out that Julio was secretive and he had few friends, and fewer still who would talk to me," He takes a bite of his lunch - a banana with melted Havarti cheese, a popular meal, he claims, in El Taupinata. Roger offers me some but I decline, as politely as I can.

"Those who did know Julio," he continues, "With the exception of two people, had only horrible things to say about him."

As if to prove his point, Roger holds up *The Bronx Gazette*, a newspaper from Julio's hometown, displaying the bold headline "SPUYTEN DYVIL DICK DIES IN DRIVE-THRU." The accompanying article is an obituary that notes that Mr. del Toro, nee Julio Van Friisjen, was born to Lloyda Delany and Henk Friisjen and grew up in the section of the Bronx, NY known as Spuyten Duyvil. The article includes quotes from several teachers and fellow students who strongly disliked him. It also includes an alleged deathbed quote from his predeceased mother blaming Julio for the destruction of her marriage to Julio's father. According to the piece, Henk told her that, after observing Julio from infancy to toddlerhood that "I can see where this fatherhood thing is going and it's time for me to cut my losses." Years after Henk left, the article said, there'd been a fire which destroyed their apartment house and injured three people. This was another incident that Lloyda had blamed her son for.

I wanted to know more about the fire. Roger, seemingly reading my mind, shows me a clipping from the *NY Daily News* with the headline, "Suspect Arraigned in Spuyten Duyvil Fire." The suspect, however, was not Mr. del Toro, but Bluet Smith. Ms. Smith, 34, an erstwhile grad student and Julio's live-in nanny, admitted to setting the blaze, which destroyed the apartment she shared with Julio, as well as the other twelve units in the complex. She had taken care of the then fifteen-year-old boy since he'd been a toddler. In the last couple of years prior to the fire, neighbors had observed the woman's mental health decline. The article included notes from a social worker's visit to Julio's apartment not long before the blaze, opining that Ms. Smith's erratic behavior was "above and beyond even the norms for this borough." The case worker had suggested that Ms. Smith undergo a psychiatric evaluation. Unfortunately, that did not occur until after the nanny was arrested.

Bluet later told police investigators that ever since she first laid eyes on the then three-year-old Julio, she was convinced that he was a wise old soul, a divine reincarnation of what she claimed were "the greatest change makers in history: the Buddha, Jesus, Mary Baker Eddy, Nelson Mandela, and the original members of [the 1990s music group] Boys II

Men." *[Boys II Men declined to comment for this article.]*

"Julio carried around so much pain because of the expectations of his psychotic nanny," Helen Waites, Julio's former fiancée, tells me via Skype. "But those two years stuck in a phone gave him more free time to process and to heal."

Stuck in a phone?! More on that later.

Ms. Waites, a stunning redhead with a self-proclaimed penchant for hair curlers, was in her car at the drive-thru that morning and saw the events unfold in gruesome detail. To her, Julio is a hero who inadvertently saved the lives of everyone present that day. She adds that when the police searched the assailant's car, they found a cache of guns and ammunition and a document titled "Grudge Bucket List" which included the names of several dozen people he apparently wanted to kill before he died. The list included well-known athletes as well as celebrities like Betty White and Drew Carey.

To this day, Helen takes umbrage at what she says are reporters' "cheap shots" when describing the man she loved.

"Sure, Julio was pretty sullen, rude even, when he first went inside my phone," she says. "But, little by little, I got to know him and he opened up to me about his father's abandonment and his mother's cruelty and stupidity. And we both cried when he said that the biggest heartbreak he ever had was over Bluet's mental breakdown and her arrest."

He confided to Helen that, growing up, he looked up to his nanny and felt that she was the only one who loved him. "Bluet convinced him from the start that he really was this reincarnated old soul and superior being. She'd talk to him, even defer to him, as if he were a wise elder, even while he was still a toddler." Most of the time, Helen says, Julio liked that. But there were also drawbacks, like Bluet getting angry whenever he didn't understand things that she felt an old soul should know. For example, Julio remembered as a young child asking Bluet to tie his shoes, only to be told to "cut the innocent act."

"It's tragic that her schizophrenia wasn't diagnosed until it was too late," Helen adds, ruefully puffing on the last embers of her cigarette. "And it really was almost too late for Julio, since, long before he realized that Bluet was crazy, she'd instilled in him a sense of superiority and entitlement that didn't serve him well in school. Or anywhere, for that matter."

I spoke with Flynn Tronski, Julio's former teacher at P.S. No. 24, who recalled his experiences with the boy. "I tolerated Julio more than his peers and my fellow teachers," he tells me. "Yet, I still think he was the biggest dickhead in all of my fourteen years teaching first grade. But I guess I should thank him. That jerk was the biggest reason I left the teaching profession and I've never looked back." Tronski decided to become a florist and move to greater Bismarck, North Dakota, where he has lived for the past two decades.

Ashauna Mann, a fellow classmate of Julio's at JFK High School (now known as JLo Academy) I interviewed, had similar bad experiences with Julio, but she too, gives him some credit. "He bullied me when I started dating a Dutch exchange student. Julio told me how he loathed the Dutch because his deadbeat father had up and left him and moved back to Amsterdam. In fact, I still remember Julio banging his desk in history class whenever Holland, windmills, or dykes were discussed." Ms. Mann's experiences with Julio's extreme prejudice, she says, led her to a lifetime of combating racism. For the past sixteen years, she's served as the Spuyten Dyvil Anti-Prejudice League's executive director.

3.

The remainder of the subjects I interviewed spoke to me only off the record. I couldn't blame them, given the less than positive things they had to say about Julio. Looking at my notes now, the adjectives most commonly used to describe him were "asshole," "dickhead," and "fuckface." A few East Coast contacts referred to Mr. del Toro as "that Spuyten Duyvil dick."

But to Helen Waites, his former fiancée, those critics didn't really understand him. Sure, her man could be confrontational and abrasive, she says, but he was more than that. "Julio was a beautiful soul wrapped in emotional doo-doo," she says. "And he was the smartest man I've ever known; a computer whiz, too!"

Indeed, Julio's technical wizardry was spotted in his first year of high school by his math teacher. The teacher (who asked that his name not be used) says he hired Julio to hack into his wife's emails to see if she was cheating. (She was.)

After that, the boy's reputation got around. Within months, he was making good money from hacking. But Ms. Mann thinks that Julio wasn't in it for the money. "It was, in his own twisted way, a moral issue," she says. Once, in their junior year of high school, she remembers Julio overhearing her talk to a girlfriend about suspicions of her Dutch boyfriend's infidelity. He offered to hack her beau's computer for free. "I took him up on it" she says, adding, "I took his offer as both an act of kindness and of hatred."

By then, Julio could well have afforded doing pro bono work. As his online reputation grew, he obtained bigger and more lucrative clients. Those were mainly small to mid-size companies that paid him well to hack into the financials of their competitors. He was well on his way to a lifetime in white collar crime.

But all that changed in his senior year when he forgot to log off his laptop and Bluet discovered how he was getting his money to buy her Beanie Babies. When she saw his illegally obtained spread sheets, her face turned a fire hot red. Her nostrils flared in righteous fury as she told him that the devil was tempting him into a lifetime of grifting when he *should* be preparing to lead the world!

Julio's reaction was to roll his eyes. He'd stopped believing that Bluet that he was some old soul messiah since the eighth grade, which was when he began to worry about her mental health. But since his mother had long since moved out and shacked up with a series of men up in Westchester, Julio was too afraid to insist that his nanny seek mental health treatment for fear that they'd have her committed and then he'd become a ward of the state.

Bluet was angrier than he'd ever seen her. She smashed a glass paperweight against the wall. Then she ran downstairs and grabbed some traffic flares out of her ancient Datsun hatchback. She rushed back to his room and lit the flares saying she had to burn his "sinful PC." Before Julio had a chance to stop her, she proceeded to burn his laptop. In the process, she also accidentally lit their curtains on fire. The fire then spread through a natural gas line in their unit shooting flames into the rest of the building. Since their slumlord—an emigre from Rotterdam—had already evicted most of the tenants to make way for a Google office, nobody was killed or seriously injured. But by the time the firefighters put out the blaze there was nothing left of the apartment house except burnt embers, molten hard drives, and the occasional scatterings of singed Barbies and adult toys.

When the police came to arrest Bluet, Julio was devastated. Now he'd lost the only person who'd ever loved and cared for him. Due to her mental state, she escaped incarceration at Sing Sing and was instead taken to the Chuck Woolery Hospital for the Criminally Insane, where she remains to this day. My multiple requests to interview her were turned down by the hospital's staff. For her own safety, I was told, Bluet has never been informed about Julio's death.

After the fire had destroyed Julio's apartment, he had to find a new home. It just so happened that Edgart Gonzalez, a fellow hacker from L.A. that he'd met online and had worked on a couple of projects together, needed a roommate. He invited Julio to come out west, saying that there were plenty of lucrative gigs spying on rival Hollywood film studios.

The next day, Julio flew out to and moved into Edgart's studio unit in Sherman Oaks. Edgart, whose own original last name was O'Malley, told Julio that a Hispanic surname would help him get business here, so Julio legally changed his last name from Van Friisjen, to del Toro, in honor of director Guillermo del Toro, whose last movie Edgart had bootlegged.

And so Julio began his new Hollywood studio hacking career. In a matter of months, his reputation for delivering the dirt on time grew and that led to him getting a steady stream of B level producer clients.

The pay was good but after a year Julio realized that Bluet had been right, he was in fact destined for far greater things. He became fascinated with 3D and AI technology and was determined to make his mark in the world through those fields.

After spending eighteen months developing his demo model - a lifelike replica of Bluet's favorite musician - the late rapper and philosopher Kanye West - Julio looked around for development funds to work out some design flaws and to get his design mass-produced. He shopped his work all over town before finally getting an interview at Muzi-Tech, a So Cal-based company that, according to its website, specializes in "connecting fans with the artists they love through personal and group 3D experiences." Though Julio had no college education (or, even a high school degree) or advanced degrees in software development, they were impressed enough to offer him an entry level position.

At Muzi-Tech, Julio toiled away for years in assistant positions. But he wanted more control in developing projects from design to production and became increasingly frustrated with merely coding tiny slices of huge pies. He thought about quitting and trying his luck up in Silicon Valley, and he even got an interview at Apple. The interviewers, however, told him that he was unlikely to make it up there, since his demeanor, they said, was too abrasive even for cut-throat Cupertino.

So Julio stayed put at Muzi-Tech, dreaming of the day when he'd be asked to lead a development team. In the meantime, he saved up enough cash to find his own digs, a studio apartment in Van Nuys. It was there that he was to meet another important woman in his life, Qez, a beautiful brunette and single mother to an eight-year-old girl named Clara.

Qez was a smart and talented apartment manager for Van Nuys Gardens Luxury Living and she tried to be a good mom. But she had drug problems especially when it came to huffing glue and freebasing cocaine. But Julio fell in love with her anyway. Thereafter, they carried on a rocky on and off relationship for four years, made even more tumultuous by the occasional appearance of Clara's dad, a feared member of an organized crime ring known as the Boise Boys.

Julio tolerated Qez's drug use and enjoyed her companionship and outstanding sexual skills, while trying to climb the so-called ladder of success at Muzi-Tech.

Everything was going along fine until Julio's world was rocked by two things: first, Qez leaving him and taking her daughter to shack up with a drug dealer and loan broker in Las Vegas; the second jolt came when Muzi-Tech hired a hotshot young coder to lead his development team, an MIT-trained engineer by the name of Alberta Stevens. Most people at Muzi-Tech liked Alberta, except for Julio, who regarded her as a was smarty pants know-it-all feminazi who was merely hired by his bosses to make him look bad.

A couple months later, things got even worse for him when Qez began calling him from Vegas, saying she needed money bad and that some South Strip sharks were threatening to hurt her and Clara is she didn't repay her loans. While Julio rejected Qez's theory that he owed her for all the times she'd had sex with him, he was sympathetic to the plight of her daughter. True, he'd never really liked the kid—and the feeling was mutual—but he remembered his own lousy mother and didn't want to wish that kind of abuse on anyone. Except maybe on Alberta.

5.

One very fateful day, Julio found a way to get even with Alberta for all his imagined slights. By happenstance he discovered that she had created the most realistic flesh and bone avatar he'd ever seen. And though Alberta had recently been promoted to Programming Head within Muzi-Tech, Julio believed that she had used the company's proprietary intellectual property to make her avatar and had developed it on company time, though she was clearly using her creation for her personal and probably perverted uses. If he could prove Alberta's malfeasance, he could get her fired. Or, better yet, maybe he could steal her coding and present the avatar—an AI version of the dead rock star Russell Aquarius - to Muzi-Tech as his own.

Either way, first he had to get ahold of Alberta's personal laptop, where he suspected the Aquarius coding was hidden, and see things for himself.

To that end, Julio hacked Muzi-Tech's personnel files and found out where Alberta lived. Knowing that she'd not be in her apartment (she'd be upstairs in another room she rented as an office) he went over to her place and, posing as a computer repairman, duped the Russell Aquarius avatar into giving him Alberta's laptop.

But before Julio had a chance to take Alberta's computer back to Muzi-Tech for inspection, she found out what happened and confronted him just as he was parking his car at the company parking lot—and in Alberta's reserved parking spot, no less. A bloody fight ensued, which ended in two gashed heads, a broken wrist for Julio—and Alberta's retrieval of her laptop.

But Julio wasn't ready to give up. That same night he returned to Alberta's place in hopes of getting his hands on her laptop again. He arrived just as Helen, her landlady, came by to complain about the noise. There was some sort of commotion going on both inside and outside the apartment and capitalizing on everyone's confusion, he snuck inside. Once he got into Alberta's unit, though, he realized that there were more people in there than he anticipated. He reached for the laptop but Alberta and the Aquarius avatar fought him tooth and nail. A brief but chaotic fight ensued whereby, inexplicably, Julio's body was descrambled and he managed to get stuck inside a cellphone.

And that phone just happened to belong to Alberta's landlady, Helen Waite. To this day, no one can fully explain how he became imprisoned in her device. All that is known, however, is that he remained stuck there for twenty-eight months until he was finally recued and released.

"Julio's descrambling was no mistake; it was meant to be," Helen tells me, lighting a Marlboro and gazing out to an imaginary sky. "That's how Julio and I fell in love. If I hadn't had sensitive hearing and had to knock on Alberta's door and shout about the noise, I'd never have met Julio, and he probably would never have zapped into my phone."

The happy accident, so to speak, led to a day-to-day relationship of sorts between the two of them, and later, a romance. Eight months into his stay in her phone, he proposed marriage and she accepted. They consulted with a lawyer to see whether they could marry immediately but were told that, under current California law, she could not marry a non-corporeal being. (Cryptocurrency lobbyists are pressing for changes to that law in light of speculators' love of Non-Fungible Tokens—NFTs, for short—but so far, the only jurisdiction to recognize purely digital marriages is the Cayman Islands.)

During the more than two years of Julio's phone incarceration, he was able to entertain himself scrolling through cyberspace, but he couldn't post or comment on anything. And, other than his new paramour, Helen, the only people he could talk to were, strangely enough, those who had other phone numbers under his cellphone plan. That meant Qez and Clara. He was determined to never speak to Qez again. But he didn't have any personal beef with her daughter.

So, when Google Calendar reminded Julio that it was Clara's birthday, he decided to give the girl a call. In contrast to all their prior communications, she seemed genuinely happy to talk to him. She was lonely. She told him she'd been left all alone while her mom took off with some people she called "glueheads" up to Boise. Through tears, she said that her mom's glue-sniffing and coke problems were getting worse, even as the woman was making more money than ever as a realtor. Julio sympathized, and told the girl of his own childhood abandonment struggles and being raised by a crazy babysitter who'd messed up his mind.

After that call, the two of them spoke every week. Helen, who'd lost her two kids in what she described as "a real estate deal gone south" back in the1980s, encouraged Julio's increasingly father-like relationship with Clara.

Finally, after more than two years of failed attempts by Helen's phone company to rescue Julio, their efforts paid off. Through some combination of complex algorithms and a freak lightning storm, Julio's molecules somehow scrambled back to their original state, and he found himself transported directly onto Helen's bed. For the new couple, that couldn't have come at a better time. Their relationship was progressing to the physical stage, and she was tired of paying T-Mobile's storage fees for keeping Julio digitally alive. Julio had somehow lost twelve pounds while he was stuck in Helen's phone, and, despite his lack of exercise, he felt better than ever.

Early the next morning after his release, Julio and Helen drove off for Vegas. Their plans were to book a weekend at Paris, Paris, and if they got drunk enough, get married there. Julio was also excited to go see Clara and have her meet his new bride.

6.

Julio, of course, never made it to Sin City. As Clara patiently waited for his visit, he was lying in a red corpuscle flood at a Taupinata Valley Jack in the Box. There's a local saying that, if a traveler gets sand in his shoes in this arid and God-forsaken place, they'll be punished by ending up staying there for life.

Along with the blood, dirt, burger wrappers, and plastic cups at the crime scene, I'll bet there were probably at least a few grains of sand in the poor guy's shoes.

Now, according to Qez, who spoke to me on the condition that I determine whether Julio had any life insurance (he didn't), her daughter has been disconsolate ever since they learned of his demise. Qez wants me to know that she's put Clara in therapy and that "despite what you may hear, therapy is not cheap." Fortunately, Helen has promised to look after Clara. The girl's even planning to say with her in L.A. this summer.

Helen tells me that her newfound relationship with Clara has helped to ease her grief over losing the love of her life. Helen adds that, of all the people she knows, her tenant Alberta has been kind and generous with her time. The young coder is even making a realistic Julio avatar designed to be an emotional and sexual companion for her landlady.

As for Roger, the man Julio inadvertently saved, his brush with death has helped him to reconnect with his troubled and estranged son, and to fund a charity for victims of drive-thru restaurant violence. And, of course, he's happily taken Gretchen, the drive-thru cashier, under his wing.

To this day, Roger tells me, his sense of gratitude to Julio is profound.

I have a hard time discerning what lesson, if any, can be gleaned from the life and death of Julio del Toro. Maybe it's that one's life, no matter how vile and despicable, can be redeemed by a single heroic act, regardless of that person's motives. Or maybe, Mr. del Toro was the right roughage at the right time to cure the constipation of an apathetic and dysfunctional society.

As for me, I'm now determined to look at assholes on freeways and organic food stores with new eyes. I never know if one of them will one day be the dick that saves my life.

THE GHOST IN THE MACHINE
By Staci Layne Wilson

Dear Diary,

Hello. My name is Alberta Renee Stevens, and I am thirteen years old. I got you for my birthday from my Nana. She says it's important to write down my thoughts and feelings with a pen on paper, and not to erase anything (or even cross it out).

She also got me a vintage Russell Aquarius poster—well, she *gave* it to me. It used to be hers. I put it up on my wall, along with my other pictures of him. I know my friends (not-friends) think I'm weird for liking my grandma's music, and Russell, but I can't help it. He was so handsome, and I love his long hair and tight pants. Mom says that's just hormones, but I don't know. Guys now, and especially guys my age, are such dweebs. I feel like I was born in the wrong time.

Well, no, I guess that's not exactly true. There were no laptops in the 1960s. The best birthday gift ever came from this contest my mom entered. It was a special drawing through her work and the prize was a computer. She won the PowerBook G4 I've been wanting! I've literally been begging for months. Which makes me wonder why I'm sitting here writing in you, when I could be playing Half-Life and adding a second boot sector for Linux OS to **<u>my new Mac</u>** ❤ ❤ ❤

Dear Diary,

Sorry I haven't written lately. I've been busy with school, and Mom has been working a lot so I have to do the housework. Yuck. Mom just opened another salon with her partner, so Nana has been here to make dinner and stuff. Anyway, last night we cranked up the Aquarius and danced on the table! (Mom, you'd better not be reading this! And if you are, don't worry… I cleaned the footprints off with soap and water and furniture polish.) She showed me how to do the Mashed Potato and the Swim (that one is funny!). I like doing stuff like that with Nana, but I don't think I'll be going to the Halloween dance at school. For one thing, nobody has asked me, and for another, I don't want to go with any of the guys in my class. Maybe me and Yuki will go, but then again… everyone already calls us "lezzies" as it is.

Dear Diary,

I'm crying right now. I had the worst day! Yuki says not to waste my energy on those jerks, but I can't help it. It was Brittany again. I <u>HATE</u> her! Her and her bony-ass friends. They suck! I had a note, so I didn't have to do P.E. I just can't stand having to wear shorts in front of everyone, so as often as possible, I say I'm sick. Today was volleyball. I know Brittany would be aiming right for my nose with those hard serves of hers. But it didn't matter. I only delayed the inevitable. After last period, I went to my locker and saw they put gum on it again. All over the combo part. Gross. Their spit was practically dripping off it. So, I decided to carry my books home. No big deal. Well, when I took the shortcut, that's when they got me. I had my Walkman on, so I didn't hear anything before it was too late.

I felt a shove from behind, and I dropped my books. They went right into a mud puddle. Then Brittany came out from behind some hedges. She was laughing at me. When I bent down to get my books, one of them took off my headphones. I think her name is Daria. Like diarrhea. She put them on, then yanked them off so fast. She broke the headset. She told Brittany and the other girl, I don't know her name, that I was listening to old hippie music. (It was Russell Aquarius, of course.) They started pretending to smoke joints and played air guitar. Not funny. They looked pathetic, really. I wanted to just run, but they had me surrounded. Besides, if I did that, it would get all over school.

Brittany came up to me, really close to my face. She said, "Oh, look, Alberta is turning red. Are you gonna cry?" I tried not to, but my eyes teared up. Gah! I was more mad than anything, but sometimes when I'm mad, I cry. I can't help it. So I said, "No, I'm allergic to dogs." That was… not smart. The next thing I knew, my face was in the mud puddle right next to my books. I seriously ate it. I even had gravel in my braces. Somebody kicked me, then they left. I got up, got my books and what was left of my Walkman, then cut through the woods to get home.

It was getting dark and it was kind of scary. The part where all the trees are isn't very big. It only takes five minutes to get through to Beeman Avenue, but you have to go by that creepy old house. The windows are all boarded up and now there's a big padlock on the front door. Some of the kids spray-painted graffiti on it, which is not cool. It must belong to someone, even after what happened there. Needless to say, I ran as fast as I could when I went by it.

Nana was there when I got home, of course, and I was so embarrassed. I was all muddy, so I couldn't lie. She gave me a hug. I took a shower, and when I was done, she made me a cup of hot chocolate and let me have a biscotti before dinner. She tried to talk to me, but I didn't want to talk about it. She tried to make me feel better by telling me about her bully troubles when she was my age, but things are different now. People are meaner. TBH it makes me never want to go to school again. I like staying in my room, anyway. I've got everything I need here: my new computer, my record player, my Russell posters, my Beanie Babies, and my books.

Dear Diary,

Mom let me stay home from school today. I didn't tell her what happened but I bet Nana did, even though I asked her not to. I told Mom I'm getting the flu. I'll deal with the gum on my locker tomorrow. Not to mention figure out how to turn myself invisible.

Nana emailed me an MP3 of a song. There wasn't a message, only the subject: THIS WILL MAKE YOU FEEL BETTER. Nana writes everything in caps, even though I've told her that means she's shouting. Anyway, I played it, and it's a Russell Aquarius song I never heard before! This is like an early Christmas! I called her right after I listened to it, and she said it's a bootleg she recorded at one of his concerts. And he only played this song once, and he never put it on an album. It's called F.E.A.R. It stands for "Face Everything and Rise." It's about not letting "the bastards grind you down." At least, that's what the song says. Easier said than done.

Later on, I'm gonna chat with Yuki on Friendster. Too bad she doesn't like Russell. She likes Oasis. I tried to tell her they're just ripping off The Beatles, but she doesn't care.

Dear Diary,

I lived another day to write to you. Maybe someday I'll look back at this book, when I'm old like Nana, and none of this will matter. But right now, it totally sucks the bongwater.

Today was the worst day _ever_. I was walking home alone again. Yuki took the bus. I wish I could take the bus without getting sick. Well, maybe throwing up on somebody's shoes would have been better than what happened.

So, I was walking home, and this time I didn't have my Walkman or any books. I even stayed late to help Mr. Singh clean up the classroom. But I didn't want to stay too late. It's getting dark so early now and I have to be home by the time the street lights go on.

I had just turned the first corner when I saw them. Waiting for me. I tried to turn around to go back to the school, but they rushed me and knocked me down. The air went right out of my lungs and I couldn't yell. I mean, I don't think I would have yelled anyway. Nobody was around and besides—if I ratted on them, they'd just kick my ass harder.

Diarrhea and the other girl grabbed me back by the arms and hauled me up. Brittany got right in my face. Her breath smelled like peanut butter. I almost hurled. She called me a biznatch and a nerd, and fat too, but I didn't say anything. She said I was a geek, which is actually a compliment, but then I did it again: I cried. Brittany laughed and said I didn't know what scared was… yet.

Her little hit squad still had me by the arms and they started dragging me towards the woods. Brittany was behind me, pushing me forward. I thought they were going to get me out of sight so they could hit me or cut my hair off or something, but it was worse than that. They took me to the house. They said it's haunted because somebody was murdered there. I didn't believe it, but that doesn't mean I wanted to go inside.

Before they put the lock on it, Satanists used to go in there and do animal sacrifices. That's why Mrs. McNeal's cat disappeared. That's what I heard. Also, Jenny's sister's friend's second cousin said that the house was made of wood from trees cut down in the

Pine Barrens, where the Jersey Devil lives, and that's why it's so evil.

The lock was pried off the door and it was open. I tried to get loose, but they threw me inside and shut the door. I could hear them laughing out there. I didn't care about yelling anymore. I begged them to let me out. I'm not proud of that, but it was pitch dark and it smelled like pee. What if there were rabid raccoons in there? Brittany and them just kept laughing and then I heard something happening around the door. I pushed the door, but it wouldn't budge. There's no knob, only a hole. I was too scared to look out, because what if Brittany had a stick or something, just waiting for my eyeball?

I didn't hear anything for a while, so I pushed the door again. It wasn't moving. So I went to the window and pushed on the plywood. It was nailed on there. My eyes adjusted to the dark, and I saw an old, nasty couch and a bunch of cigarette butts and roaches on the floor. And cockroaches, too. It was so cold I could see my breath on the air. I tried calling for Brittany and whoever, but they were gone. They just left me. I asked myself, "what would Gordon Freeman do?" but then remembered he's just a character in a videogame. Playing Half-Life hadn't taught me how to escape a haunted house, after all. Then I thought, "What would Russell Aquarius do?" That made me smile, because I bet he would have smoked those roaches and wrote a song about it.

I decided to check for a back door, and that's when I heard somebody say something. It sounded like "boo" which is totally cliché, but it wasn't

Brittany, or anybody outside. It was inside. I asked who was there, then I saw this blurry flash, like a ghost. Then the dark corner had an even darker thing in it, like a black hole. Like something was growing, gathering itself into a form, taking shape from the shadows. I closed my eyes so tight I saw bright spots, but when I opened them again, it was still there.

There was no back door to the house, so I tried to open the front door again. I even ran at it with my shoulder, but it didn't work. It looks so easy in the movies. I didn't know what to do, and the couch was way too gross to sit on, so I just stood there. In a while, probably only a couple of minutes, but it felt like two hours, I heard "boo" again and saw the blurry flash. This time, I didn't ask who it was. I knew it was a ghost. The Ghost. The murder victim, out for revenge on the living. But it didn't scare me this time. I said hello, and I introduced myself. There was no reply, but just knowing he was there gave me an idea.

By the time I had my idea all worked out, the door opened. I mean, all by itself! I ran out, and then booked it all the way home. It was past dinnertime, and Nana called Mom, and Mom came home. They were just going out to look for me.

This was when I had to weigh my options. Tell the truth and have Mom go to the school and everything, or say I lost track of time and be grounded? I chose the latter. Being grounded is hardly any punishment for me. It just gives me more time to work on my idea. I'm on restriction for three days. The Halloween party at school is a week away, which gives me just about enough time.

Dear Diary,
It's 3 a.m. I heard that same voice from earlier, and I saw the blurry flash in my room. The ghost followed me home.

* * *

That was the last entry in Alberta's diary.

Anyone finding it later on might think the worst. But as the ghost himself, I can assure you I did not hurt a hair on that pretty little head.

After hanging around that creepy old house for so long, I was bored. I mean really, *really* bored. But what was there outside for me? At least the house provided a credible backdrop for my boos and rattling of chains. I've scared so many mortals away, I think I might hold a record of some kind. Even the stoners and vagrants who wandered in to party or get out of the rain were never confused about whether I was a hallucination—they knew death when they saw or heard it.

Alberta was the first person that asked me who I was and she even introduced herself. This was different. She was smart and inquisitive. Also, the City had demolition orders to wreck my house. I wasn't sure where I'd go after that. But then I got an idea. So, I followed her home.

I wanted her to know I was there, so at 3 a.m.— I use time to my advantage; that and midnight seem to hold some sort of significance for the living—I whispered her name and I started doing that gathering darkness thing in the corner by her closet.

She sat up in bed and narrowed her eyes. They found me quickly. Her breath caught, then held. She was scared.

Then she spoke (quietly, so as not to wake her mother across the hall), and I realized she wasn't scared at all. "Hello, ghost," she said. "Why are you here?"

Alberta then produced her diary from under her pillow and wrote in it. She was documenting me. I was flattered, but I also wanted her full attention, so I rustled around a little.

In the plus column, I wasn't bored anymore. This was the most excitement I'd had since I crashed the set of *The Exorcist*. In the negative, now I had to come up with something better than the routine specter shit. My moans and chain-rattling weren't going to cut it.

Besides, I really didn't want to scare this kid. So, I decided to answer her question. I moved forward, and sat on her bed. She saw a depression from my weight—all an illusion, of course, since I have no physical body. Her eyes widened, but with curiosity not fright. I projected my words into her mind, and she received them readily.

She replied, using her voice. I explained to her that we could both communicate telepathically.

"Whoa, cool!" she said (without saying).

"I think so, too," I agreed. "But after all these centuries, it's old hat to me."

"Centuries? You mean, you're not the guy who, uh, died in the house in the woods?"

"I've got news for you, kiddo," I replied. "Nobody was ever murdered in that place, and the wood-siding does not come from the Pine Barrens. It's from The Home Depot. I made all that up to create a legend. What's a ghost without a legend? The real reason the place has been vacant for so long is that its owner abandoned it and forgot to mention to her family it was even there. She died without a will, and the place went to the City by default. Needless to say, I'm pretty up on elder and estate law."

She contemplated this. "Why were you there, then?"

I was still invisible, but I shrugged anyway. "No reason. I guess you could say I'm a squatter."

"Wait. So… ghosts don't haunt the places where they died?"

"Some do, probably. Me, I just liked the place. I prefer to be alone. It's so annoying trying to coexist with people. Families, especially. The ones with kids are always trying to banish you. If I smell one more branch of burning sage, I swear I'm gonna lose it."

"Yeah, I can imagine that would get pretty annoying." She crossed her legs under the blankets and settled in for a chat. There was no way she could go back to sleep now. She glanced down at my butt-cheek impression on the edge of her bed. "If you have mass, why can't I see you?"

I took a moment to compose myself. Literally. I arranged my essence in such a way that I could be seen. I chose my favorite version of myself, from when I was in the prime of my life. I put on modern clothes, right down to the sneakers on my feet. It still took a little effort to do this. But I'd improved quite a lot in my skill—at first, I'd made a few mistakes. I'd appear without clothes, or I'd be in whatever my current corporeal state was (decomposing at first, then nothing but a grinning skull). I then explained to Alberta that I do not have mass, but I liked to pretend that I did.

"Fascinating," she said. "So, you're like a hologram?" She reached out, and her hand passed through me.

I laughed. "That tickles."

"Really?"

"No, not really. I just like to pretend."

"So do I." She reached over to her nightstand and opened her laptop. "In fact, I'm making a hologram right now. Wanna see?"

I shifted my vision to her screen.

She pointed to the code. "In case you don't know, a hologram is kind of like a ghost. It's a recording of an interference pattern which uses diffraction to reproduce a 3D light field, resulting in an image which has depth, parallax, and perspective that can change according to the angle."

While I found her tone somewhat condescending, I did appreciate her intellect. I'd never encountered such a smart child. And, I felt sorry for her. Those girls who'd locked her inside my house were real bullies. I knew from reading her thoughts that she was making this hologram to use it as a revenge tactic.

She caught me reading her mind. "So, I guess you know I plan on using this at the Halloween dance to scare Brittany and her bony-ass friends. But I have two problems. First, I don't have a model. I was going to use myself, but I don't think I'm scary enough. Secondly, I need a laser light to project it."

She was smart, but not as smart as I'd originally thought: the answer to her problem was staring her right in the face. To illustrate my point, I made her see me as I looked when I was in the third stage of decomposition. This is when the maggots hatch to feast on a carcass's festering flesh. Bloated tissue liquifies, and then disintegration sets in. Plus, I stank. *Bad.*

She coughed in disgust, but she caught on quick. "Oh, I could model my hologram after you!"

Almost. "No," I said. "I can *be* your hologram, all by myself. Skip that slog, lose the laser, and let *me* scare the piss out of those girls! It'll be fun!"

Alberta contemplated this. "How do I know I can trust you to come through?"

"That's rather cynical for someone your age," I groused. "But I get it. You'll just have to trust me."

I hung around for the next week, and watched as Alberta made her hologram. Not only was she hedging her bets, she actually enjoyed doing all that work. After she perfected her masterpiece, she backed it up on an external drive. In spite of the show, I sensed that she had decided to trust me. After all, I hadn't vanished yet.

* * *

The night of the Halloween dance arrived, and the weather was perfect. It was as wet and gloomy as I'd hoped. Alberta was going dressed as the Jersey Devil, which was, of course, our inside joke and a wink to my little fib about my former abode being made from Pine Barrens wood. She'd brought her laptop in a backpack, just in case. I tried not to feel insulted.

I floated around unseen (and unsmelled—I decided to store up the putrid stench for later) in the car with Alberta and her mom, who was dressed as a riské witch. Perhaps not the best costume choice for a school dance chaperone, but who am I to judge? On their way, they paused to pick up Alberta's friend Yuki, who'd chosen to go as a giant frankfurter. She said she'd have the scariest costume of all, "because everyone knows what hotdogs are made of."

The gymnasium was the site of the party, which was just about to get started when we arrived. There were black balloons all over the place, green and orange streamers, punch bowls wafting plumes of dry ice, and all the foods that hyper teens shouldn't be eating—candies, cakes, cookies, and the like. The place smelled like a giant gym sock and the pop music blaring from tinny speakers was enough to send me hurtling for the nearest grave.

To say I had fun that night would be an understatement.

Our plan began partway into the festivities, after a few dances. When Brittany, Daria, and Karen were at the punch bowl, Alberta stood nearby, announcing loudly to Yuki that she was headed to the girls' room and that she'd be right back. Yuki, who was not in on the plan, said she'd go with.

"No," Alberta nearly shouted, "I'll be *right* back!"

Brittany, who was dressed as Baby Spice, turned around and said, "Oh, are you sure you don't want your *girlfriend* to go with you?"

"Buzz off," Alberta replied, "I'm just going to test my hologram."

Brittany crossed her arms. "You are such a nerd."

Alberta shrugged.

"What's it for?" Brittany asked.

"You wouldn't understand. But it's something I made for the end of the party. We're showing a video."

"How stupid." Daria (Sporty Spice), rolled her eyes.

"Yeah," Karen (Posh) echoed. "Stupid."

"Whatever," Alberta sighed, then headed for the bathroom.

As predicted, the bullies couldn't resist the chance of getting Alberta alone with all those filthy toilets. They followed her quietly so they wouldn't attract the attention of the adults, but anyone paying even a whit of attention would see the prey/predator dynamic.

Alberta stepped inside, then when directly to the third stall. She shut the latch, then crouched on the toilet seat so that her feet couldn't be seen by anyone looking under the door.

The trio were close behind. As soon as the door closed, I killed the lights. They were in total darkness. Immediately, Brittany turned and shoved on the door, but needless to say, I'd locked them in.

Then my fun began.

I'm not one to give away trade secrets, but suffice to say it was a job well done. Daria slept fitfully with all the lights on for the rest of her life. Karen joined a nunnery five years later, taking on the name Sister Annunciata. My crowning achievement was, of course, the ringleader Brittany. Although I don't like living with families, I made an exception in this case, setting up camp underneath Brittany's bed. She suffered from various nervous disorders and was eventually committed to the Happy Gully Sanitarium in Camden, NJ. Brittany was released at the age of thirty, and went on to become an unsuccessful writer of horror novels.

Several Years Later.

Alberta Stevens Case Study
Gloria J. Trallis, PhD., CA Psychologist License #00492
May 2025

The patient is convinced that she met and interacted with a sentient ghost when she was thirteen years old. In the 1970s, '80s, and '90s, it was common for pubescent children to invent fantastical stories and poltergeists to explain and justify confusing or stressful life events.

As such, the adverse situation may stem in part from a so-called broken home—38% of case studies by the De Palma Institute of Parapsychology involved children who did not live with both parents. In Alberta Stevens' [hereinafter referred to as 'A.'] case, she never knew her birth father, and her mother was overprotective yet absent much of the time due to work.

These phenomena manifest as the mischievous actions of a discarnate spirit or demon, reflected in the historical use of the term: poltergeist. [German for 'noisy spirit.']

This particular incident involving revenge on three bullies on Halloween night is noteworthy, as it may relate to the subject's fascination with the rock musician Russell Aquarius, who was killed in 1970 via electrocution from a faulty microphone while performing onstage. According to A., she and her grandmother enjoyed listening to his music. Interestingly, A.'s grandmother passed away shortly before A.'s psychosis and paranoia were brought to my attention.

According to A., her protective poltergeist locked herself and three other children [names redacted] inside the girls' bathroom at their school during a Halloween dance, then proceeded to traumatize A.'s tormentors using visuals, noises, and scents; no physical harm was inflicted. A. claims she does not know the current whereabouts of said ghost.

Further study is required.

OH, HELEN!
By Nancy Long

The metal cuffs pinched her wrists and the chains around her ankles clanked as Helen shifted her weight from side to side, the shag carpet sticky between her toes. There was a small, rectangular, window directly across from her. But someone had quickly taped it up from the inside so that only a pinprick pierced the darkened room and cast a narrow shard of light across her soft nipples.

It felt like she'd been standing in that warm, dank, room for hours and she was getting drowsy. And hungry.

"Hello," she said to the empty room. She scrunched her nose and struggled to scratch it on her shoulder. The tickle only grew. She squatted then, bending forward to try to touch her face to her knees. But, with her hands locked securely behind her back, the motion almost landed her on her backside. "Hello!" she repeated, louder this time. Helen struggled to stand again. "Help me!" she cried. "Help!"

Sounds came from the next room. She could hear the old door rattle and shake. Someone was fiddling with the knob but it wouldn't turn. "Shit," she said under her breath. Then a few big thuds and the door flew open.

A young man in a tattered motorcycle t-shirt and faded jeans stood just inside the doorway. He rubbed his shoulder and waited for his eyes to adjust to the dim light. He looked over at Helen and smirked. She was wearing nothing but panties and suddenly felt self-conscious under the boy's scrutiny.

"Hurry up! I'm dyin here…"

"What d'ya want?"

"Would ya come here?"

"Harry said not to go near you."

"I'm just askin…"

"You wanna get me fired?"

"No, I just need you to—"

"What?"

"My nose."

"What about it?"

"It just… It itches! It's drivin me crazy!"

"Yeah, well you yellin at me to come in here every two seconds is drivin *me* crazy!" He turned to walk back out the door.

"Wait!" Helen tossed her feathered, auburn hair and smiled as he turned around. "Be a doll and itch my nose for me?"

"Scratch."

"What?"

"It's *scratch* your nose. Pretty sure it already itches."

Helen cocked her head. "Okay, Professor. Then scratch it. I'm gettin crazy here!"

"*Gettin* crazy?"

The young man made the universal sign for cuckoo, his finger circling his temple.

"Oh, come on!"

He crossed his arms and sighed. "What'ya gonna do for me if I do?"

She looked at him coyly and smiled her most seductive smile. "You scratch my nose and I'll scratch your, uh, y'know..." She winked, and he smiled a big, toothy grin.

The young man walked slowly toward her. He was shorter than Helen by several inches and had to carefully reach up to scratch her nose. Helen moaned in relief. He grew visibly excited.

"Come a little bit closer—you."

"But, Harry said…"

"Forget Harry, oh, mmmmm… Yeah, that's it."

She moaned again and the young man moved close enough that she could smell the stench of cigarettes and Bubble Up on his breath.

He cupped her left breast and closed his eyes as he leaned in. But the clank of chains at his feet startled him, and he opened his eyes just as Helen slipped her ankle from the manacle and kneed him square in the balls.

He yelped like an asthmatic dog and fell to the floor writhing in pain.

"Now go tell fuckin Harry that I'm tired of standing around. He still owes me from yesterday, and I'm charging him double overtime for today."

The young man could hardly hear her over his own sobbing.

A moment later, Harry, a lanky, hirsute, man in shirtsleeves and baggy suit pants appeared in the doorway.

"Oh, Helen." He shook his head slowly then snickered. "What the hell didya' do that for?"

She shrugged.

"That's the third kid this week."

The boy whimpered and crawled out of the room.

"Yeah, well, maybe you should stop hiring such pervy little creeps. Besides, I'm tired of waitin around. Let's get this show on the road!"

Harry looked over his shoulder and then nodded toward the ancient piece of equipment sitting in the middle of the room. He spoke in a hushed tone.

"I thought I told ya already. This camera's, well, it's pretty jacked…" His voice trailed off.

Harry thought of himself as a visionary. An idea man. It wasn't in his purview to have to worry about the little things like how to actually make a film. But, apparently, no one else bothered to worry about it either. They were too busy vacuuming things up their nose.

Helen closed her eyes and leaned back against the wall. It was always something or someone that was broken.

Except Helen. Unlike the torrent of pretty girls pouring into Los Angeles, she had a plan. Helen wanted something real, something lasting. After watching her mother drown in Tab following the heartbreak of yet another Publisher's Clearinghouse scandal, she took the first Greyhound and headed west. This whole acting thing was just temporary: A means of scraping up enough of a down payment to get her own place. Maybe even an apartment building or two. The only sign in Hollywood that interested Helen was one that read "Private Property."

Harry cleared his throat. Helen opened her eyes and stretched her long, lovely neck. Her auburn curls grazed her collarbone.

"Besides, shouldn't you suffer for your art?"

"What? You get me out of these fuckin cuffs and I'll show you some suffering, if you catch my drift."

"Now, there's my girl."

Her voice cracked, "I'm serious, Harry. And I'm *not* your girl. You promised me this job would be different!"

Harry moved toward Helen and gently brushed her hair from her face. He looked into her eyes and traced his finger along her neck and down her chest. Then he jumped quickly away, narrowly escaping the knee that was meant for his left nut!

Harry laughed. "Ya still got it! Ya still got spunk!"

"Yeah, well, you're not gonna have any spunk left when I'm through with you."

"Ah, darlin don't say that. We're making somethin beautiful here."

"Beautiful, my ass!"

"Now that you mention it, it truly is a thing of beauty. In fact—"

Helen frowned. "Don't you say it. I told you, I don't do the..."

Harry looked like he was enjoying himself. "The what, Helen? What don't you do?"

He took her by the shoulders. "Don't you wanna be a star? You could be the next Linda Lovelace!"

She shook her head adamantly. "No, no, no! I already told you!"

"But that ass! You've got a million-dollar ass. We could be rich!"

"What'dya mean 'We', White Man?"

Harry looked hurt. "I thought we were a team?"

"Yeah? Well, I don't see you standing around naked for hours with your hands tied behind your back."

"But darlin it's different for me. I'm the director. You just gotta be patient."

Helen stepped out of both of the ankle chains and sat down on a stool next to the broken camera. "Patience, my ass."

"There you go talkin about your scrumptious behind again. Me thinks m'lady doth protesteth too much!"

Helen wriggled hard, squeezing out of the handcuffs and flung them at Harry. They clipped his left ear and dropped to the ground with a hollow clank.

"Ow! What the hell?"

"I'm tellin you, Harry. Lay off or I'm gonna take this sweet ass and walk right out that door."

"Okay, okay. Jeez. I'm just tryin to make your dreams come true."

"This?" Helen glowered at the moist, dark room. "This was never my dream."

Harry shook his head. "Come on, doll… Stop shittin me. You know as well as I do that every beautiful girl dreams of coming to Hollywood and seeing her name up in lights."

"Except that's not my *real* name up there on the marquee next to all of those Xs, is it?"

"Is that what this is about?"

"What?"

Harry knelt before Helen and stroked her cool thighs with his large hands. "Look, I know that this isn't as glamorous as you'd like, but you gotta pay your dues…"

Helen pushed his hands away. "I've done nothing but pay dues my whole life. It's time I got a little somethin in return."

Harry parked his hands in his baggy trousers and shook his head. "So that's it, huh? I shoulda known. It's always like that with you broads. All you want is money!"

"Isn't that what you want?"

"It's different for men."

"Really? How so?

Harry smiled so his teeth showed. But his eyes were steady and cold. "You know, for every pretty little girl who thinks she's worth a million, there's twenty more willing to do whatever it takes, whatever *I* want them to do, to become a star. And let me tell you, I've seen plenty of uh, how you say, *delectable* derrieres…"

He looked over his shoulder. Music was coming from a record player in the next room. Helen had always been sensitive to noise, but she didn't mind the sound of Russell Aquarius's music. *Furry Freak* was like a crazy ear worm, and she couldn't help humming along under her breath.

Harry looked back at Helen and smirked.

"'Matter of fact, I've got two of my own little, ah, furry, foxes waitin in the next room"

Helen stood up unrestrained and ran her hands through her hair, knotting it behind her head.

"See the trouble is, I do know what I'm worth. But, I also know what *you're* worth, Harry."

Harry stopped grinning. "What the hell's that supposed to mean?" He looked back over his shoulder to make certain no one was at the door.

"It means my ass is smarter than you think. I know how much you're worth and I know how much you owe!"

"I don't owe you a goddamned thing!"

"Not me, you moron! Although, come to think of it…" Helen laughed and wiped the Abstract Orange lipstick from her mouth with the back of her hand. "You see, I know you've promised a lot of investors a lot more than you can deliver. And I also know you've been spending too much money on coke, and booze, and all those other pretty, little girls…"

Harry stood up nervously. "What the hell are you getting at?"

"I just think your investors would be real interested to know that Mr. Harry Rosen is, uh, how you say, insolvent? And then they'd probably like to know where all their money's gone!"

"You little witch! If I'm so broke, what is this then?" He reached into his pocket and held up a thick fold of bills. "Besides, you wouldn't dare!"

She shook her head. "Try me."

Harry shoved the money in his pocket and slowly backed out of the room until his body filled the doorjamb.

Helen bit her lip and gave him a lopsided smile. She dangled the heavy ankle chains behind her back. "That's where you're wrong about me, Harry. I mean, I never wanted the things you thought I did. I never wanted stardom!" Helen walked slowly toward Harry keeping him in her steady gaze.

"Sure you did. You all do."

Harry ran his hand along the door and felt for the doorknob. He froze at the sound of his baggy sleeve as it caught on the lock, then struggled to free himself.

Helen sniggered seeing his arm awkwardly pinned behind his back. Now, maybe he'd know what it felt like. "Naw, Harry, with this brain, and this um, ass… I'm a lot more clever than those other girls."

With that, Helen flung the long chain like a Ninja's Kusari-fundo and unfurled it against Harry's jaw, knocking him backward. His shirt sleeve ripped as he slid to the ground, his lip split open and blood oozed down his crumpled suit. Harry spit on the floor and wiped his bloody mouth on his other sleeve.

Helen stood over him, her long legs straddling his twisted ones.

Harry cringed waiting for a second blow. "Okay then. What the hell *do* you want, Helen?"

She paused for a moment, then reached down and grabbed the wad of bills from his pocket.

"What do I want, Harry? I'll tell you what I want." Helen grinned. "Real estate."

FIST THROUGH THE GLASS [The Unseemly Coincidence Regarding My Eyepatch]
By Sid Greenblatt (as told to) Martin Olson

Into the pit of the page, we go. For the record, my name is Sid Greenblatt, President of Greenblatt AAA Talent Agency, which I started with a desk, a chair, a phone, a Rolodex, and eighty bucks in my pocket, more than thirty years ago. I was asked to contribute an account of my relationship with my favorite and most lucrative client, rock star Russell Aquarius. Russell died young. When I heard the shocking news, I sobbed like a baby. Poor talented kid. But even in death, he made me a ridiculous amount of money because, publishing.

You've seen that crazy story plastered all over the news, the story of his resurrection. But I'm here to tell a different story, the strange and rather disgusting tale about, while saving him from a crazy person, I received my eyepatch as a present.

Russell's great singing, songwriting, and headline-grabbing stunts were making him an underground sensation. Thousands of spoiled-rotten kids flocked to see him. By the late '60s, every show was sold out. I'd just booked him in The Bomb Factory, the best rock venue in Dallas, when Crazy

Dallas Chick, aka Claudia the Stalker, reared her pretty little head again. She'd been sending Russell increasingly insane, scary, fan mail, mail that I intercepted and never let him see. But Crazy Dallas Chick's fan mail was so insane and scary that I put a restraining order on her, banning her from any future concerts. Besides, Russell had an exclusive attraction to very short girls, and the stalker was on the tall side and wore heels, which turned Russell off like a light switch. (I personally love heels on a woman but to each his own.) Anyway, I made a point of handing every security guy at The Bomb Factory Claudia's name and photo so that when they checked IDs at the entrance, they'd kick her out. My security chief was dependable and everything was set.

That spectacular venue, by the way, was an actual converted bomb factory. And that night, the atmosphere fit its history, for the room felt explosive. Onstage, Russell was like a rock and roll god on fire, and the packed crowd was eating it up.

But other things soon became explosive, especially for me.

In a clever disguise and with a fake ID, Claudia the Stalker got past security and managed to sneak backstage. I soon learned that she wanted revenge on Russell for banning her, even though he knew nothing about her and the whole thing was all my doing.

Luckily, or not, I was alert and spotted Claudia backstage. She looked completely different in a black wig. But she looked gorgeous. Through the crowd in the wings, I saw her surreptitiously remove a jar of what I later learned was battery acid from her jacket, unscrew the top and start towards Russell onstage. I quickly pushed through everybody, grabbed her hand holding the jar and, as we struggled, the battery acid splashed into my face. As I screamed and fell to the floor, clutching my eyes, Claudia surprised me by kneeling next to me, crying and apologizing. She felt terrible about my face and clearly had forgotten about her revenge scheme. As she held me, she screamed for somebody to call an ambulance. She rode in the ambulance with me to the hospital, and stayed with me there the whole night. They tried to flush my eyes out with saline, but found that my right eye was destroyed. They surgically removed it, and adhered a patch over my socket with gauze and surgical tape. An appointment was made to have my eye replaced with a glass eye.

Claudia was definitely insane, but there was something about her. She held my hand all night as I slept in the hospital bed, and in the morning kissed my forehead, repeated her sincere apology, and quietly left.

The next day, upon leaving the hospital, I got a message to meet Claudia for a drink at her favorite watering hole. As we sipped old fashions in the dive bar, she revealed that she was a sex worker. She explained that she had fits of PTSD due to events in her past, felt enormous guilt at what she'd done to me during one of her uncontrollable fits, and offered to take me back to her place to try to make it up to me.

I'm not a complete idiot. I know my brain was

deluded by booze and from anesthetics and pain killers from the hospital. But that night in the bar, communing so honestly with Crazy Dallas Chick, she slowly transformed into something quite extraordinary. Through my one remaining eye, I began to feel her every look and every word as emanations from the heart of an angel. I was beside myself. Claudia was truly the loveliest and sweetest creature I had ever met.

Now you know the set-up. Therefore, bear with me while I crack open my literary journal, from thirty years past, when in my spare time I was publishing highly literate short stories under a pseudonym in classy rags like *Colliers*, *The Saturday Evening Post*, and *New York* magazine. Just go with me on this. Here is what I wrote back then about what happened, with precise descriptions, laying them out as they occurred, beat by incredible beat:

The evening sky was squeezed by our drunken perceptions into an intense rainfall. As we departed the filthy bar, both inebriated, also intense were our torsos, inflamed with lust. At least, I should clarify, mine was. Through the torrential Dallas storm, she led me through the night in elliptical arcs, in an ever-widening gyre, betwixt a crumbling hodgepodge of labyrinthine alleys, at the center of which lay her apartment, which I shall call the Minotaurean flophouse.

I followed her in a daze, aware that, alack, this was a peregrination of potential perdition; in other words, I remembered her letters to Russell and considered that the evening might end with me being stabbed with a clam knife. However, despite the fact that I am responsible for my every action in this vale of tears, in one sense I was blameless on that particular evening, for the real culprit was the magical energy called love, beaming like an etheric rope from my eyes, twining about Claudia the Stalker's heart and, vis-à-vis, dragging me along like a flopping Howdy Doody through the serried swath of streets.

Anon, she led me to the flophouse. Stepping over a bad-smelling obstacle course of sour-wine-stupored indigents, we entered through a filthy glass door, bedecked with a gay, expressionistic design of mauve spittle and chartreuse phlegm. We approached the front desk inhabited by the next person on our roster of introductions, the hotel clerk, soon to be described in the adjacent paragraph.

The clerk in question, by happenstance, wore not an eye bandage but a legitimate, black eyepatch, as sported in the past by sailors, pirates, and criminals. He was a very short, very strange-looking man whose one visible eye, upon seeing me, creased into deep suspicion. This, in combination with his rather grotesque, angular face, gave him the appearance of a cubist portrait, comparable to the ugliest of Picasso's *Three Musicians*.

At the desk, Claudia seemed to transform again, this time into a woman with a much harder edge. She indicated that I should pay the clerk twenty dollars as a tip. She then explained that she would go up to her room and request that her roommate, of whom nothing is known in this story, other than the implication that she, too, was a professional, vacate the premises for one hour. To this end, Claudia requested of me another twenty dollars to appease her roommate's sensitivity to her encroaching physical displacement. These duties I faithfully discharged, whereupon she assured me that she would return shortly, pecked me dryly upon the cheek, and swaggered, her buttocks undulating rhythmically to an imaginary snare drum and hissing high-hat, as she swaggered into the nightmare graffiti of the elevator.

I was thus left alone, my clothes and eye bandage soaking wet, as the clerk glared at me, staring specifically with his visible eye at my bandaged eye, shifting restlessly from one foot to the other, scrunching his tiny features into a one-eyed sneer.

I, therefore, avoided his burning gaze and affected drumming my finely-filed fingernails upon the grimy counter in an attempt to counterfeit a savoir-faire attitude of careless panache.

This lack of attention on my part towards one so accustomed to being a formidable magnet of curious stares served to drive the tiny night clerk out of his already questionable stability of mind. In response to my voided gaze, the angry clerk slapped his stubby, outstretched hands on the outer edge of the counter and, like a homunculus gymnast, lifted himself by his arms, inch by inch, inclining his sneer up, up, towards my torpid features, until his ghastly breath beat upon the receptive pores of my nape, and reflexively shut them up like ten thousand tiny trap doors.

I reluctantly turned my head forward towards the offending halitosic breeze, and distastefully lowered my gaze to meet, eye to yellowed eye, with the sneering, furious stump of night clerk flesh.

In the first inaccurate draft of this biographical record, I wrote that here I attempted an obviously puerile parlay to dispel the psychic tension inflicted upon me by the gymnastically-inclined, tiny man; in this, the final draft, however, the brief and boring conversation precipitated by my inane query has been omitted, due to a lack of space, and, chiefly, interest.

It was here, upon this page of my remembrance, as distilled here dryly on the page, when I am verily eye-to-eye with the seething clerk, that another profound insight flared and supernovaed in my skull-cavity:

This insight was, indeed, as profound as that experienced when I first gazed into the eyes of my newly-found beloved, Claudia the Stalker, save that in this second experience with the clerk, the expansion of awareness was mental, not emotional. For here, within our eye-to-eye stare, I suddenly experienced an epiphany regarding the intimacy of the moment, in that of all the human souls which had graced or polluted the wobbling gyroscope of the earth, out of these unnumbered trillions, perhaps, here was I in momentary communion with a specific one-out-of-a-trillion; and the materially unexplained intuitive faculties holographically enmeshed in my mind made it plain to me that such a selective intimacy was not a chance operation, but rather it felt to me that the cretin in effect symbolized a portion, or reflection, of my own consciousness; and although I could not prove it, certainly not with the kindergarten crayons of logical analysis, I felt, in the innermost point of my being, that in looking into the eyes of the tiny clerk, that I was looking into the eyes of a portion of myself. This was not something I could prove; rather, it was something I knew.

This ingenuous intuitive perception ricocheted with lightning speed through the recesses of my subconscious like a manic pinball through a pinging machine. Although my conscious assimilation of this insight appeared minimal in light of my later adventures, still my subconscious assimilation was as vast as my inner being itself, rippling as a stone's radiating waves through a crystal pond, subtly permeating my every subsequent encounter, imbuing them, great and small, with a profound significance, in the oceanic expanse of my secret, spiritual existence.

Perhaps my interesting insight would have been more apparent upon the skein of my personality, if the link of my eye with his eye had not been interrupted by the homely opening of the elevator door, and causally-related (?) appearance of Crazy Dallas Chick approaching me and brashly informing me that, indeed, the spatial rectification concerning the occupancy of her room had been completed, as a preface to raw sexuality.

As a result, soon I was propelled in an incongruous mode of motion; namely, my body moving straight up into the air at a uniform rate, by means of the graffitied elevator mechanism, which appeared in my mind all at once as the evolutionary modification of the primitive structure of stairs, which I dully surmised cumulatively occupied tens of thousands of square miles, across the face of the earth, if laid side by side, or stair to stair, as in a mental paradigm, not unlike imagining rows and rows of pairs of tits, of the girls one has laid or potentially laid, in matter or in imagination, splayed out geometrically in cubic grids of tits, large and small, firm and sagging, those volcanoing milk and those barren, those hairy and those devoid of hair, square acres of tittage mathematically carpeting the crystalline surface of the universe, like self-replicating cellular automata, ultimately making all of infinite space itself nothing but tits, tits, tits, tits, tits, tits, and tits.

This boring thought concerning tits, in my brief hiatus from reason, was gladly interrupted by the shuddering halt of the elevator in its ascent and the whirring opening of the elevator, a glimpse, in my drunken mind, of the future evolution of the primitive structure of doors, although, it must be noted, that the cleaving of the doors, as it were, also reminded me of tits.

I nervously shuffled behind the measured slither of her previously described protruding buttocks as she reached her room, inserted a symbolic key into the room's tiny secret opening, and bade me enter.

Now enclosed within the confines of Claudia the Stalker's lair, I must abandon, it appears, my passive, self-effacing conservatism and contrive to enthusiastically mount her in the manner of a rapacious young bull.

Yet, this configuration was not to be. For as Crazy Dallas Chick stripped off her layers of petroleum-based garments with mechanical rapidity, the polyester blouse and skirt going *hweeesssh-hweeesssh* like a toreador's cape flourished towards a horned beast, I stood at the foot of the bed watching her, suddenly lost in my thoughts and unable to make a move.

Trained in her years of anything-goes coupling, Claudia, in observing my seeming complacency, did not pause to ponder its significance but rather exhibited a long-practiced facial expression indicating insatiable sexual hunger for the purpose of arousing my sagging, bovine-like torso junk to rigid and turgid attention.

Yet I couldn't, and merely stared at her. Intractable, motionless.

Claudia, a professional sexual psychologist, inquired whether or not I would like to insert the appendage of my manhood into the sluicing hollow of her feminine mystique.

There was the usual long pause, as long pauses are wont to crop up in any show biz manager's mundane life, with exponential frequency, as I waft through these linear corridors of my memory, a professional waftee, as it were, writing in search of immortality through the non-linear portals of descriptive literary adventure.

The empty interlude had run its course. I

decided to boldly speak my mind; I would forgo attempting to rationalize my feelings and alternatively allow my words to simply spill forth, going where they will, whence I knew not, only that they issued forth. By this medium, then, I emptied my heart thusly:

But to quote my speech at this juncture would be a cruel invasion of my privacy and the privacy of Claudia the Stalker, for they are not words of love, intuitively rushing from the lips to the air, viewed at a more reserved moment in time, when they may lie naked as frozen words on the page, seen then as foolish homely splutterings, instead of the sacred truth from a realm in the heart too real to be borne by words alone? Are not the words on paper akin to dry desert bones which once housed the vital immediacy of living, loving flesh?

As I stood there babbling to myself, I began to speak, baring my soul to Claudia there at the foot of her bed, expressing my feelings with words that could not fully contain my meaning. And my meaning was that I loved her, that I loved her with such profundity of feeling that I pledged, then and there, vaguely in the manner of a knight of the Middle Ages, to dedicate my life to loving her. Furthermore, I expressed the novel and exhilarating realization that my love for her was entirely nonsexual, that perhaps (given time and assimilation) I could eventually consummate our love via the symbolic act of sexual congress. But my feelings at this point were so true and so intense that I wanted only to vow my undying love and adoration, to spend quiet evenings with her in intimate, atmospheric, overpriced restaurants, to travel the world with her in First Class, where you could ask the waitress or waiter in the sky to cook the asparagus more fully so that the stalks are not so raw and stringy, and otherwise to fully experience with my new-found love all of the joy, wonder, pain, disillusionment, and puerile meaninglessness that human life has to sweetly offer, with her and her alone, to hold her perfect, tattooed bodice tenderly in my arms, and then—

At this point in my idiosyncratic (and rather self-absorbed) speech, Claudia the Stalker pointedly interrupted me by shrilly shrieking a caustic two-word phrase, beginning with the sixth letter of the alphabet and ending with the twenty-first.

Her shriek served to shut me up quite nicely, and I stood, stunned, watching her throw her clothes angrily back on, while casting me the vilest of looks, accompanied by loathsome epithets of disdain. For of all the noxious, ancient sympathies and humors to which Claudia had been resignedly subjected in her sex-working career, the most noxious to her personal temperament was the *jejune* client who, at the moment of truth, preached the heresy of Platonic Love.

Reader, I was crushed by her bald negativity. As she reclaimed her scattered rayon sheaves from the gritty sheets while muttering fiercely as to the questionable polarity of my masculinity, I courageously summoned up my presence of mind to desperately remonstrate as to my total sincerity and, indeed, my intention to be joined in holy matrimony with her, once my present marriage to Carole Anne, my high school sweetheart, who had fallen in love with a Pasadena pastry chef, was duly renounced and adjudicated.

This proposal of marriage, however, instead of attracting Claudia to my emotional sphere, served to repel her even more violently than before. She jumped off the bed, screaming ancestral Portuguese invective, her otherwise beautiful face, now blackly caricatured by crevasses of skin tensely bunched together over her eyes, inches from that of my single working eye, punctuated her furious remarks with jabs of her sharp, cleft chin towards my heart.

Again gathering my courage, I valiantly attempted to reinforce and elaborate on my argument. But there was barely a moment for me to insert a single word, for Claudia was rife with sluicing rhetoric which foully and rapidly emitted, machine gun-like, from her lipsticked, Eolithic lips.

Thus was I dolefully rebuffed in my quest for romance.

As I steadfastly refused to depart without further restating my case to my beloved, in rebuttal, she extracted a clam knife from her purse, fulfilling my previous premonition, and viciously sliced the air back and forth in front of my swollen eyepatch.

Hweesh! Hweesh! went the clam knife.

I backed out through the door in fear of obtaining an unnecessary skin graft by an obviously untrained surgeon, who at this very moment on the page uses her past stalking skills to threaten me, her blade hissing through the air and her breath hissing through hatefully clenched teeth.

Backed out, out of the room, into the cheap decor of the hall, I observed Claudia's door loudly slamming in my pallid face. I stood there hearing her still-ejaculating lips scream bitter diatribes at my memory. Truly, I did not know what, at this juncture in time, to do. There was nothing in my Hollywood managerial bag of tricks that knew how to deal with this colorful but violent, romantic rebuff. For here, in the distinctly urine-besotted hallway of the flophouse, I stood bereft of all objects of my desire, psychologically castrated of my manhood. I knew only that I would not storm the gates of her chambers, for a number of ethical reasons; this, for example, would not be indicative of the air of supreme self-confidence with which I usually command myself, in both my successes and failures.

True, I had fallen in love with Claudia, and loved her more than life itself, but not more than my need to avoid being stabbed with a clam knife.

Remember, my patient reader, that this is me, Sid Greenblatt, not some random knucklehead devoid of professional prowess and life experience. There will be time later for me to lose the need to save face, to surrender my personality, the last bastion and stronghold of all seemingly individual humans, against the great emphatic, gentle (?) unity of All That Is.

I, however, was firmly resolved to eventually win over my beloved whom I unconditionally adored. But for the duration, I must reluctantly leave and allow her to become used to the idea of being loved. So that I might contact her again, at a more auspicious time, and eventually ask her to be my wife.

Yes. At that moment, standing in the urine-scented hallway, that was my long-term plan.

I turned, pressed a button, and entered the evolutionary machine previously described and traveled downward in a simple-minded symbolic descent that we need not waste paper on, not even about tits, for let us keep this in perspective: if you are reading this in a paperback book, as opposed to reading from a screen of light, then a noble, living tree was slaughtered so that we may, in fine, tell this ineffable story, of what was to be my life-long love for Claudia the Stalker.

But returning to the matter at hand, suffice it to say, I exited the electronic portal and passed again by the tiny night clerk, whose former arrogance had vanished utterly. For now, to my surprise, he was weeping on the front desk, sobbing soulfully, his eye-patched head buried in his tiny arms. Behind him, the old-fashioned telephone receiver was dangling and swinging by its old-fashioned cord, as if thrown in mid-sentence by a caller rife with rage and despair.

Not perceiving me perceiving him, nor the Reader perceiving me perceiving the clerk, nor an omnipotent and insane Universal Creator perceiving the Reader perceiving my story--unless they are all, of course, the same Cosmic Personage in different bodies—the tear-stained clerk screamed in anguish, again getting the Reader's attention, which has been somewhat distracted due to an excess of literary verbiage and a lack of literary action. In a fit of sorrow, the screaming clerk grabbed a framed photograph from his desk and furiously smashed his tiny fist through the glass, ripping asunder the photo, a tatter of which wafted downward, like the pendulum-like motion of falling autumn leaves, amid shattered glass and shreds of cardboard, to my feet.

I stooped over and retrieved the photographic shards and, piecing them together on the counter, saw in amazement the subject of the photo.

It was an image of my client, Russell Aquarius.

It appeared that, somehow, the clerk had a physical or platonic, homosexual bond with Russell, either from afar or through a physical connection unbeknownst to me. Since I knew of Russell's preference for very short women, it was possible that he secretly also enjoyed very short men.

The weeping clerk grabbed the photographic shards from my hands, stared at the pieces of Russell through his tears, then at my bandaged eye. And then he did something completely unexpected. Whimpering that he only wore the black eyepatch because Russell found it attractive, he ripped the eyepatch from his face, revealing two perfectly functional, tear-stained eyes. He thrust the eyepatch into my hands and said, "I think you need this more than I do." Then he resumed weeping into his arms.

I gingerly backed away, walking backwards towards the exit door, holding the clerk's eyepatch, thinking to myself, since I could think to no one else (?), that the coincidence concerning the photo, recurring like a refrain, had it not actually happened to me (?), would have seemed, in the literary sense, forced and contrived to the extreme. But as it had just actually happened to me, I had no recourse but to accept this coincidence at face value and dream of a better, brighter day, having better adventures in a better blather of words, in better stories to lift my spirits from the doldrums of my mundane profession.

But let us not become bogged down with literary criticism from the central character, myself, in the midst of my travails, for now, even as I carefully step backwards over the artistically-arranged tableau of sleeping winos cradled in Claudia's flophouse doorway, we must faithfully contrive to get me back, back to my own apartment, wherein my unfaithful wife Carole Anne innocently sleeps, dreaming of Pasadena croissants, as my tale of the unseemly coincidence regarding my eyepatch, and the clerk, and my poor boy Russell, and the stalker I love, thankfully, and with finality, reaches, at last, the end.

THE CASE OF THE SINGULAR MAN

By Darren Gordon Smith

Dr. Sterling double-checked the locks on her office door. At night, the crusty 1950s era fake rock-face medical building that housed the Wellness Mindful Help Clinic and its poorly-lit carport made her feel uneasy, especially on evenings like this when she was the only one left in the office to see new patients. And to add to that, the guy she saw tonight *really* gave her the creeps.

Plus, on top of goosebumps, she also had a massive headache. Ever since she woke up this morning every nook and cranny in her cranium pounded rhythmically, radiating eighth notes of pain.

Dr. Sterling popped a couple more Motrins and gulped them down with her vat-sized bottle of Evian. What she wouldn't give to be curling up with her tabbies right now, sipping warm chamomile with pistachio milk, and catching up on a psych journal or two! But first, she needed to type up her notes while her mind was still fresh.

She studied her notes from this evening's session as though they were hieroglyphs. Even as a girl, her scrawl had always been barely legible. In fact, her parents used to beam with pride at her strange cuneiforms, saying that with her illegibility she had the makings of a doctor. She grew up to earn a Ph.D. instead of an M.D. and all the while her handwriting got worse.

When she held her notes close and squinted, she still couldn't read everything but luckily was able to get the gist. Just in time, too, for the fluorescent lightbulb above her that had been cutting in and out in the past month since she worked here, made a sound like a bug lamp zap and dimmed for good.

In the dark, illuminated only by her monitor, in hunt and peck style, she typed:

> Merrick McGillicutty (MM), age 36, no history of mental illness, made first consult, complaining of irrational ideations and fears for his safety. Possible signs of psychosis. Fears that his girlfriend Alberta (A) will "terminate" him (his words) by "uploading his soul to the cloud." Patient concerned that he is not really human but rather a computer simulation.

> MM says that his ideations started three months ago after an accident in which he suffered several electrical shocks. He claims no physical injuries from the accident other than painful sensitivity to bright light. He did not seek medical attention, saying that A downplayed the incident, though he has been convalescing ever since at her apartment. MM complains of "overprotective" girlfriend forbidding him from leaving the apartment

without her. He says he's sometimes allowed to leave the apartment at night so long as A accompanies him. Even then, though, they only go for short walks around the block.

Patient says that, probably due to his electric shock, he has no memory of any events from the past three years. He says that his memory is otherwise good and he can vividly remember people and places going all the way back to childhood.

Patient has been seeing girlfriend for past eight years "on and off." He says that A is a self-described "recovering agoraphobe" but he is unaware of any other mental health issues she might have, past or present. MM says that his relationship with A was "excellent" prior to the accident but "horrible" since that time. He describes her caregiving as "obsessive" and has been depressed since the accident, mainly owing, he says, to A's insistence that he take a leave of absence from his work (he is a cosplay event planner) while he recuperates.

He added that the only reason he was able to make tonight's appointment was that A had left for the evening to go to a party and wouldn't be back until late. She did not invite MM to go along. MM slipped out of the house just after A left. Throughout our session, MM frequently checked his watch saying that he was nervous about getting home before she finds that he slipped out.

When asked whether he had "snuck out" before, MM nodded and said he started to get out last week, while A was out in the afternoon and evenings volunteering for her pet charity, Tech for Tots. Because of his extreme light sensitivity, he has been waiting until sundown, and even then, avoids looking at car lights or neon signs.

Patient cannot provide further details about his alleged electric shock since he says that he has no memory of that incident. A told MM that she came home from work one day (she works in an upstairs vacant apartment) to find him lying face down on the floor of her apartment, unconscious, and holding a frayed lamp cord. He has no recollection of how long he was there and why he was even at A's house to begin with.

I advised patient to seek medical care in order to determine any long-term physical damage. MM refused, claiming that A would find out and "kill" him. He doesn't know A's reasons for discouraging him from seeing a doctor and that she "flew into a rage" when he inquired about getting x-rays.

As to A, he says he does not remember her having anger problems until after his accident. MM worries that her outbursts have been becoming more frequent since the accident and her threats toward him more ominous.

Yesterday, MM said that A caught him out on his nightly walk. She dragged him inside and said "this is the last straw" and that if she caught him out again, she would "store him away." Moreover, ever since his accident, A had joked that he was an android that she created for her sexual pleasure. Due to her frequent demands for intercourse MM now thinks she wasn't joking at all.

I asked MM how he felt being used in this way, he was silent and first, and then admitted "it makes me horny." When I couldn't help noticing the growing bulge in his pants, I abruptly stopped this line of questioning.

Instead, I asked MM why he believed that A wielded so much power over him. He responded that she held the power of life and death not only over him but also other men, most notably, the legendary musician Russell Aquarius, whom she allegedly resurrected from the dead.

MM added that A also had something to do with a business rival "getting stuck" (his words) in her landlady's cellphone. When confronted with the irrationality of these superhuman feats, the patient became defensive and angry. He banged the armrests of his chair, and called into question my experience and background as a therapist. He questioned my Chicago School of Professional Psychology degree, wondering whether Midwesterners have the kind of interpersonal skills needed to be effective therapists. Though I allowed that there was some merit in that way of thinking, I steered the conversation back to the issues at hand.

MM began to cry. Through barely muffled sobs he told me he was certain that A's threats to "turn off and store" him were not merely speculative but certain. And, they were also imminent.

At this point, I informed him that our session was over. We booked him to come in next week. I told him to be prepared to talk about possible self-esteem issues as well as other relationships.

Suddenly, from outside came a flicker of lightning followed by a crash of thunder. Dr. Sterling looked out the window but saw no rain. It's not like anybody was expecting it. After all, the broad-shouldered so-called meteorologist himbo on this morning's news didn't forecast rain in L.A. for at least another 45 days. She made a note to start watching the big-breasted bimbo weather girl on Channel 2. Though outside it was still dry, a fog wafted in, making the parking lot right below her window look darker and more dangerous, even by East Hollywood standards.

She thought about the feel of Merrick's cold hands as they shook goodbye. And how seeing his eyes up close gave her a chill: the hollowness of his stare, as if he had no corneas and his eyeballs were merely holographic projections. But the look of fear on his face, saying he had to rush back before his girlfriend got home "or else," made her feel less scared of Merrick and more sorry for him.

Dr. Sterling recalled how years ago her brother had been in an abusive relationship and no one believed him about his violent wife, much less helped him, and by then it was too late. The doctor couldn't let this happen to Merrick!

She checked her calendar. Merrick's next visit was scheduled for the following week but she now thought he should come in at least twice per week, at least for the time being.

She took out her cell and dialed the number he'd given her. All she got was a computerized female voice claiming, with digital glee, to be sorry that the line was no longer in service. She looked at the number again to see if maybe she'd misdialed. She hadn't.

As other desperate people do these days, she turned to Google. On her laptop, she searched for "Merrick McGillicutty." Google yielded thousands of entries, and according to one site, Spokeo, there were 144 of them in California alone. She found a Martin McGillicutty living in L.A., but the thumbnail pic showed a skinny ginger Caucie that looked nothing like the patient she saw tonight, who was Black and, in her view, attractive.

Dr. Sterling decided to try a different approach by doing some digging on Merrick's alleged girlfriend. The doctor searched for "Alberta" and "Russell Aquarius" and found two articles from five years ago about rumors that an Alberta Stevens had something to do with Russell's reincarnation. According to the articles, she worked for Muzi-Tech, a virtual reality company based in Sherman Oaks. In another piece, it was noted that Alberta was an expert in the burgeoning field of Singularity, a complicated field that theorized the merger of man and machine. Dr. Sterling did some further research on Singularity and read things about the futurologist Ray Kurzweil and immortality through digital storage and AI before realizing she was going down a rabbit hole.

Instead, she called the number she found for Muzi-Tech and asked for Alberta. The receptionist, a gruff-sounding woman who seemed wholly unsuited for a people-oriented job, said that "the chick" no longer worked there. Dr. Sterling asked her whether she knew where Alberta had gone to, the woman said no, asking rhetorically, "You think I got a LoJack up her ass?"

Dr. Sterling was about to hang up until the surly receptionist said, "Hold on, lady." After a few minutes on hold while listening to an instrumental loop of "We Are the World" fourteen and a half times, a man came on the line (less of a man and more of a bro, actually) and said that a guy who used to work there was dating Alberta's landlady, a woman named Helen Waite, and maybe this Helen would know. He gave Dr. Sterling the woman's number.

Dr. Sterling dialed Helen and told her she was looking for Alberta. Helen said that she never gives any contact to anyone, "even cops," about her tenants, especially Alberta, who Helen described as noisy but a good tenant. Though Dr. Sterling knew that she couldn't straight out divulge any patient confidence following her meeting with the alleged Merrick, she implied that she was Alberta's doctor, that she couldn't get ahold of Alberta, and that this was very serious.

"Gosh," replied Helen, "I hope she's alright." She proceeded to give the doctor Alberta's cell number.

Dr. Sterling steeled herself before calling Alberta. She wasn't sure what she was going to say nor did she relish the possibility of getting into a verbal spat with this controlling and undoubtedly unpleasant woman over Merrick. The doctor's headache was bad enough as it was without having to deal with Alberta, but she was concerned for Merrick and took her job seriously.

She dialed the number and the phone rang. Then it rang some more.

One more ring and she was about to hang up, when Alberta finally picked up the phone. Alberta apologized for not picking up sooner but said she hadn't heard the ringing over the Russell Aquarius music she was blasting while doing housework. Dr. Sterling was pleased with the woman's apparent politeness and amiability. Of course, Dr. Sterling had come across plenty of manipulative "nice" people well before becoming a shrink. And she was especially wary after seeing a picture of Alberta, knowing that, in the doctor's personal experience, the beautiful ones generally did the most harm.

Dr. Sterling told Alberta that she'd seen a Merrick McGillicutty in her office and his phone appears to have disconnected and asked Alberta for help tracking him down. Alberta said she didn't know anyone by that name.

The doctor was incredulous, though she couldn't say why. She asked whether Alberta was sure.

There was a pause and then Alberta laughed. "I think I'd remember an unusual name like that."

Dr. Sterling thanked the woman for her time and hung up.

Now she was back to square one. And her headache was getting even worse, like tiny little jackhammers of pain drilling into her cranium. She rubbed her temples and tried to think. Why had Merrick, or whoever he really was, concocted some elaborate story involving Alberta Stevens as the villain? Sure, crazy people say they're Elvis or Oprah or Bob Saget all the time, but this was different.

Of course, like many grad students in her chosen field, Dr. Sterling studied cases of schizophrenics who believed that The Beatles or Loggins & Messina were controlling their minds. But most of these cases involved older patients who'd been chewing peyote for years. Though the man who called himself "Merrick" was younger and did not otherwise exhibit symptoms of schizophrenia or drug abuse, could it be that he'd heard about these older patients and seized on their paranoia as his own?

Sure, she surmised, it was possible that there really was some *actual* link between Merrick and Russell Aquarius, but it was equally likely that Merrick had a random psychotic obsession that was as inexplicable as Hinckley's with Jodie Foster, or Trump's with Obama.

She sat back in her chair and thought through her conversation with Alberta. The woman had been nice, but maybe almost *too* nice. Something in Alberta's pause when Dr. Sterling had questioned her about Merrick felt strange.

The doctor tried a new search, Googling "Alberta Stevens" with "Merrick McGillicutty." The search yielded nothing of value until she saw a picture of Alberta Stevens with her arms around the guy who looked *exactly* like the patient Dr. Stevens had just seen! She clicked on a link for the guy, which went to the Facebook page of someone called "M.M. Macgillicuddy". There, she saw smiling pictures of him in numerous cosplay costumes with various people and what appeared to be more recent shots on the beach with a young redhead he called his fiancée. At the bottom of the page was another photo of M.M. Macgillicuddy with Alberta in cosplay costumes captioned "TBT – Memories at *RepoOperaCom*'17."

Macgillicuddy's Facebook page had a hyperlink to his LinkedIn page. Dr. Sterling checked that site and saw that another picture of the man and said that he ran a cosplay consulting business in Tampa, Florida. His CV showed a bunch of prior cosplay-related jobs, and most of them had been in the L.A. area. This had to be the guy! Fortunately, he'd posted a business phone number.

She dialed the number. She expected to leave a message but the man picked up on the first ring. He'd been asleep—she'd forgotten that it was well past midnight Florida time – but picked up thinking that it might be his fiancée calling from London. "3M" as he said that he liked to be called now, was equally as personable on the phone as Alberta had been, despite having been woken up. When asked about his name change, he told Dr. Sterling that he'd changed the spelling of his last name to reflect his roots with the MacGillicuddys, a Black Irish clan. He added that he also had always hated the name "Merrick."

She started to try to explain the purpose of her call. Therapist/patient confidentiality rules prohibited her from divulging any communications, but she had to say something. She mentioned Alberta Stevens, to which 3M cried, "Oh, God no! Is she okay?!"

While trying to reassure him that Alberta was fine, as far as she knew, she was forced to tell him, at least in general terms, about a guy who'd come into her office claiming to be Merrick and claiming to possibly be a computer simulation.

As soon as she said this, 3M let out an audible sigh. He said that he'd broken up with Alberta three years ago, that the split had been amicable, and that since he relocated to Florida he'd gotten engaged to another woman. And yes, the redhead in the pics was his fiancée, a Disneyworld performer named Corriandra. He told Dr. Sterling that "he'd take care of this Merrick problem," though he refused to elaborate when Dr. Sterling asked what he meant by that.

She thanked him for his help and ended the call.

Suddenly she heard the BOOM of thunder and a white flash of lightning illuminating the night sky. This time, the rain finally came. In buckets.

She unlocked the bottom drawer of her desk and took out the cash that "Merrick" had paid her with. She held the three crisp hundred dollar bills to the light of her laptop monitor. They had watermarks and appeared real. She wondered why someone would waste an hour of their time and $300 to make up this elaborate story about avatars, domination, and Singularity. If this guy were lying and had some private beef against Alberta, why would he come to see her when nearly everyone knows that therapist privilege barred her from doing anything about it? Why wouldn't the guy just go to the police? And since this "Merrick" guy otherwise appeared healthy and had a job to go back to, why didn't he just move out? Of course, the same question could've been put to Dr. Sterling's brother before he was killed by his wife. Obviously, things weren't so simple, which is one of the reasons she became a shrink in the first place.

And what if this guy had been telling the truth, that Alberta planned to "terminate" him? The adage "just because you're paranoid doesn't mean they're not out to get you" came to her mind. Clearly, this guy she saw had some serious psychological issues, but what if Alberta really *was* threatening him? Maybe she slowly was poisoning him and/or making him slowly go mad? But why? If Alberta was playing dangerous psychological games with him, what did she get out of it, other than maybe playing out freaky Frankenstein-like fantasies? Dr. Sterling would have no way of knowing unless maybe Alberta came to her as a patient. Even then, Alberta's motives might still be a mystery.

Just then, her phone rang. It was 3M calling her back. He said he just called Alberta and "straightened everything out." He said he couldn't go into any more detail than that. He added that the doctor need not fear that this impostor would ever contact her again.

When Dr. Sterling asked if he knew why Alberta had denied knowing Merrick McGillicutty, 3M said he didn't know, but he was quick to add that if Alberta had said it, she must've had a good reason to do so.

Before ending the call, the doctor asked 3M what he knew about the science of Singularity. Not much, he claimed, other than saying he knew that the goal in that field was the ultimate merger of man and machine and, through Alberta, had met a few "nuts" who were trying to upload their consciousness into the digital cloud and, through AI technology, achieve some sort of immortality. But 3M said that even if he knew more about what the tech experiments Alberta may have been working on were, he wasn't authorized to say anything more. And, when pressed about his knowledge of 3D virtual creations, he got angry, said he "knew nothing about avatars" and hung up on her.

Why did 3M mention avatars? she asked herself. And really, what the hell *is* an avatar, anyway?

Those answers would have to wait for another day. Dr. Sterling's now full-on migraine was making her dizzy. She put the finishing touches on her report, closed her file, and logged off her computer. She turned the lights off, locked up, and walked down to her car in the driving rain.

She looked around warily before getting in her car. She even looked in the back seat before getting in, as if—just like almost every crime show she'd ever seen—some creep was just sitting there waiting for her in the dark so he could put a gun to her head and strongly suggest that they "go for a little ride."

Of course, there was no one in the back seat. (Or was there?) Exiting the parking lot, she hit a massive puddle and her head pain and blood pressure exploded. Before pulling out, she wiped the fog off her windshield. It barely made a difference. It was dark as hell and there was zero visibility. The rain turned into hail which bounced off her car like BB pellets, the sound reverberating like machine-gun fire in her head. She braced herself for the long drive home.

TRUST NOBUNNY
By Staci Layne Wilson

Russell Aquarius woke with a jolt. He looked around the unfamiliar room, waiting impatiently for his bleary eyes to adjust. He sat up, then went prone as a dizzying headrush claimed his balance. "Ughhh…" he moaned. "Not again."

Bright stars of static electricity sparked from the pillow to his hair, making his ears ring more than usual. As a rock musician, ringing ears were par for the course—but it didn't usually last for more than a few hours after a gig. *How long have I been asleep?* he wondered.

He remembered getting onstage at the Gettysburg show, but that was about all. He cut his gaze to the space next to him. He was alone in the bed. Another rarity. He tried to sit up again, this time more gingerly. His brain went on the whirligig but soon righted itself. He took a deep breath, coughed up hash-phlegm, then turned on the bedside lamp. Yep: another hotel room. They all blended together after a while, but he recognized the Continental Hyatt House when he saw it. *Hmmm.* He was in California, nearly 3,000 miles from Pennsylvania.

The Hyatt was his home away from home, ever since it opened seven years earlier as the Gene Autry Hotel. Now, in 1970, it was affectionately known as the "Riot House." Rock bands had coined the nickname because they could trash the rooms, hurl television sets out the windows, and ride their motorcycles up and down the halls with little consequence (other than the inflated bills for damages).

Russell's room was intact. *Slow night.* He threw the covers off and saw that he was wearing the garish tie-dyed briefs made for him by one of the groupies, Mary Juana. That, and a fringed suede vest. His feet were bare, and he didn't see shoes or any other clothing nearby. Not that such accouterments concerned him.

He got up, swayed with rubbery knees, then stumbled into the adjacent bathroom. His travel bag was not there, but thankfully the hotel had provided some toothpaste. He brushed with his finger, then gargled, banishing the burning hash residue from deep inside his throat.

He went to the phone and called the front desk. It rang and rang. No answer. Next, he made a call to his manager, Sid. Once again, his call was ignored. Unusual, but not unheard of. Russell quickly grew bored of his own company, so he decided to take a look around to see if the rest of the band was next door. They usually rented the whole floor.

Russell went to the door, then realized he didn't remember where he'd left his key. To be on the safe side, he decided to prop the door open with the Gideons Bible from the nightstand drawer. He stepped into the hallway and looked left to right, then back again. It was not only dark, but there was a strange, chilly breeze in the air. Russell shuddered and rubbed his bare arms to warm them. He ventured farther out. He heard the door to his room click closed, in spite of his precaution. *Should have used the Koran*, he thought.

The door across the way opened, and a warm, inviting light spilled out. "Come in," someone said. The sweet, inviting sounds of an acoustic guitar could be heard, as well as female laughter.

Always up for a party, Russell grinned and stepped across the way. No sooner was he in than the door slammed shut behind him. The room was bathed in an ethereal golden glow, and Russell had to squint to make out the four figures that stood before him. Like a camera lens adjusting to its subjects, they slowly came into focus; there were three men and one woman.

Russell instantly recognized the shaggy blonde mane and kindly countenance of his friend Brian, guitarist and sitarist of The Stones. The two had bonded a few years back at a love-in thrown by Ravi Shankar after they discovered they both smoked the same brand of cigarettes.

"My man!" Russell laughed, grabbing and hugging Brian.

Brian hugged him back, then introduced his companions. The soul brother with the inviting smile was Sam; the elderly, bald-headed white dude with the crazy eyes was Aleister; and the fifty-something chick in the white dress with long, flowing sleeves and a big Christian cross embroidered on the front was Aimee.

Russell had been there when Sam debuted his song *A Change is Gonna Come* at the Troubadour five years before, but had yet to meet the man. He wasn't sure who the two old squares were, but his brain was treading water—he knew he'd seen them somewhere before.

Aimee handed Russell a fat doobie, then turned to face the room, where somebody was playing a Martin D-28, and two pale, nude groupies were on the bed, braiding each other's hair.

"Cool scene," Russell said, accepting a light from Sam. Russell flopped onto the bed, then took a long, lung-punishing drag from the joint. "Ahhhh," he sighed. "Better."

"Where have you been?" Brian asked, sitting cross-legged on the floor.

"On tour," Russell replied. "I did an Independence Day gig at Gettysburg, and…" He searched his memory and came up empty. "Well, then I ended up here." Another thought wafted into his mind. Something very bad had happened a year ago to the day… but what?

He shook his head and took another toke. Unbidden images seared his mind's eye—a gun, a pile of pills, and a pair of disembodied black lungs, all sinking to the bottom of a swimming pool—then a giant lightning bolt obliterated everything into a puff of smoke.

Russell flung the flaming spliff across the room. "What's in this? Angel dust?!"

"Angel?" Aleister shook his head vehemently. "I shall not tolerate such blasphemy!"

"Blasphemy?" Aimee shouted at the bald septuagenarian. Her eyes blazed. "I shall have you know, sir, that to be empty of self and be filled with Himself is my mission."

"You've come to the right place," Russell winked. She was ancient, but still hot.

Aimee smiled serenely at him.

"Well, I don't have to listen to this!" Aleister blurted, but stood his ground. The room was small, after all, and there was no evident retreat for the huffy old man.

"Oh, yeah?" Aimee's smile turned upside down.

"Now, now," Sam soothed, putting a calming hand on each of their shoulders. "We're having a party for Russell here, remember? Be cool."

Russell looked at the smoldering joint on the floor with regret. He got up and retrieved it. He looked over at the man playing the Martin, but he couldn't make out his face. It was… blurry. "I have one just like that," Russell said. "Great sound." The guitarist just ignored him, so Russell shrugged and reclaimed his place on the bed. He looked at Sam. "A party for me? Why?"

"Why not?" Brian responded.

"Yeah, why not?" Russell echoed, chuckling. He got the joint going again, and flinched when the cherry hit a cluster of seeds, sending sparks all over. He brushed away the embers.

The young women on the bed were no longer braiding each other's hair. Now they were mixing something up in a large bowl with a whisk. He took a whiff. Plaster of Paris. "What's that for?" he asked them. They giggled in response. "Ohhhh," he said. "You must be Plaster-Casters." They just kept whisking.

Russell lay back on the bed, and said, to no-one in particular, "I always wanted to be cast. I mean, they got everybody who's anybody. I'm somebody."

"What, pray-tell, is a Plaster-Caster?" Aimee asked, sitting on the edge of the bed.

"They're a group of groupies who make molds of their conquests," Sam said, cutting Russell off.

"Of… what?" Aimee asked.

"You know. Jimi's wild thing, Wayne Kramer's wang. The Band member's members."

Aimee gasped, covering her mouth. "Oh, my!" Then she cut her gaze to Russell, zeroing in on the bright red tie-dye heart on the front of his briefs.

"Why would they bypass you, young man? Looks like you have a lot to offer for art's sake."

Russell nodded. "I know! The truth is, they tried. I'm usually harder than Chinese algebra, but that night I'd had a scare… and a bad one."

"What happened?"

"Crazy Dallas Chick."

Aimee cocked her head, not getting the reference.

Brian got up from the floor and sat beside her, then Aleister joined. The bed was getting crowded. Russell didn't mind. The more the merrier.

"She's a fan. She threw battery acid at me earlier that night while I was on stage in Houston. Happened a few months ago, I guess." Russell had retreated to the Salton Sea where he camped out for a week with nothing but STP and a bag of magic mushrooms. When he returned, Sid, now sporting an eyepatch, assured Russell that "CDC" wouldn't be bothering him anymore. Russell assumed Sid had paid her to go away, or maybe she shaved her head and joined a Hare Krishna cult.

"That was a dark scene, man, but it's all good," Russell continued. "I'm doing my tour of famous battlegrounds, and I'm here now, with you guys and this righteous weed. All's well that ends well."

Brian, Sam, Aimee, and Aleister looked at each other.

"Um, Russell?" Brian ventured. "There's something you need to know."

"What?" Russell grunted, having just bogarted the last of the blunt.

"All done!" shouted one of the groupies, holding her mixing bowl aloft. "Are you ready, Russell?"

Russell sat up. He looked at the girls, but didn't recognize them from his last encounter. "Who are you, anyway? Were you there after the Houston show? The Dallas show?"

"We're not the Plaster-Casters, silly," said the paler of the two. "We're the Ball-Busters!" she held up a giant nut-cracker and cackled hysterically.

Russell froze in horror as everything around the room fell away into darkness. Brian, Sam, Aimee, and Aleister drifted away into a purple abyss. The bed was now floating in deep space, and Russell caught stars and distant planets swirling in the periphery of his vision. The groupies hugged each other, then melded into one undulating gelatinous mass. They turned to liquid, leaving nothing but a sticky splotch on the polyester comforter.

Russell shoved himself up against the headboard and grabbed a pillow, clutching it tightly to him like a shield. He squeezed his eyes shut. *I'm just having a bummer trip, that's all. I'm okay, you're okay. This tape will self-destruct in five seconds…*

Russell felt a jolt, then a hard landing. His spine quivered. Fearfully, he opened one eye, then the other. The bed had landed in a meadow surrounded by a serene forest. Cool, spring-scented air enveloped him, and he could see the late afternoon sun low in the cirrus-spotted sky beyond the treetops. He exhaled and let go of the pillow. Beneath the bed was tender young grass, and above in the branches, Russell heard gentle birdsong. He righted himself, and let his legs dangle from the side of the bed. He was about to stand, when movement caught his eye.

Something was coming out from under the bed.

It was a baby rabbit. Russell's heart stalled, then began to thump furiously. Another rabbit darted out, and then another. There was a flood of them— bunny after bunny, until they were nothing but a blur of fur and endless ears.

No, no, no… Not again. The worst trip of Russell's drug-addled life came rushing back: a ginormous lop-eared rabbit with glowing pink eyes had chased him from the Whiskey a Go-Go all the way to the Avalon Ballroom. As a result, he'd become seriously angoraphobic. He'd even canceled his subscription to *Playboy*, stopped eating Trix cereal altogether, and sold his stock in Nestlé Strawberry Quik.

As if bidden by Russell's bad memories, a mammoth hare half-hopped, half-lumbered from the woods, knocking trees out of its way with its short forelegs and leaving rabbit-foot craters in the earth like something out of a bad fifties kaiju flick.

Russell had to crane his neck to see to the tips of its ears, which were touching the clouds. The rabbit snickered, exposing sharp incisors. The creature came closer, casting a dark shadow over the bed. The air chilled, and the smell of shredded carrots filled the air. Russell hunkered down, steeling himself for the inevitable footfall. He shut his eyes and prayed to Robert Johnson, the patron saint of rock 'n roll.

He waited to be crushed.

And waited.

There was no sound, no smell, no movement.

Russell opened his eyes.

The rabbit was not gone. It stood next to the bed.

Russell saw a rope ladder dangling from the rabbit's kangaroo-like pouch. It ended at Russell's feet. He looked up—the rabbit gazed down at him with a benevolent expression on its otherwise terrifying rodent face.

Russell understood. "You want me to climb up?"

The rabbit gave a single nod.

Russell shrugged, then took hold of the ladder and made his way up it. He marveled at the downy softness of the fur against his bare feet as he braced himself on each rung. Finally, he made it to the top.

The pouch opened, inviting him. Russell peered down into the blackness, and an aroma that reminded him of his mom wafted up. He missed his mom. Having been orphaned as a youngster, he barely knew her, but he remembered her perfume, and that's what the pouch brought to mind—a lavender-scented womb.

He held himself up by his fingertips at the inner edge of the pouch, and then he let himself go. Flashes of 1's and 0's filled his mind. There was a barrage of electronic voices yelling at him: *You've got mail!*

Then there was nothing. He fell head over heels, spinning round and round in darkness for some time. As he fell, Russell grew drowsy, and then he succumbed to the deepest sleep he'd ever enjoyed.

Russell woke in a strange bedroom to the malignant death rays of daylight. He hated mornings, always had, even well before his ascent from folk clubs to Filmores East and West and all the psychedelic blues joints he'd played in between. In fact, unless he was puking up peyote in the desert while hallucinating coyote gods, he pretty much didn't like daytime at all.

But at least the nightmare was behind him. He looked at the girl sleeping beside him. She had long, light brown hair, and a rosebud mouth—she was obviously an admirer, as she was wearing a psychedelic Russell Aquarius tee-shirt that looked like a bootleg, or in any case, non-official merch he'd have to ask Sid about—and she was very pretty.

Russell reached under the shirt and stroked her warm body.

From her dreamy haze, she responded in kind.

This is nice, he thought. *I think I'll stay awhile.*

About the Authors:

Brooke Lewis Bellas is an actor and author. She plays Tawny Stevens in *The Second Age of Aquarius*, and is an executive producer on the film.

Nancy Long is a singer and writer. She produced *The Second Age of Aquarius*, and plays the role of Helen Waite.

Martin Olson is a comedy writer, television producer, author, and composer. He plays the role of Sid Greenblatt in *The Second Age of Aquarius*.

Darren Gordon Smith is a screenwriter, film producer, author, and songwriter. He cowrote and produced *The Second Age of Aquarius*, composed the score, and wrote the vocal songs.

Staci Layne Wilson is a writer and filmmaker. She cowrote, produced, and directed *The Second Age of Aquarius*.

About the Film:

Synopsis. Ever wonder what it would be like to bring your favorite dead rock star back to life? Alberta certainly has. Since she was a kid, she's dreamed of a world where ultimate '60s rock icon Russell Aquarius was still alive and writing songs just for her. Now a successful computer programmer, she takes her fandom and wishful thinking a step further and makes a Russell Aquarius avatar. Her loneliness and a freak power outage give her more than she bargains for when sparks fly not just in her computer, but also in reality when Russell's avatar comes to life. Alberta is played by Christina Jacquelyn Calph, and Russell is played by Michael Ursu. [Poster design by Aaron Kai.]